Table of Contents

LOSING MY WIFE TO ANOTHER MAN 3 INTERRACIAL CUCKOLD LOVE STORIES

PETE ANDREWS
(WRITING AS XLEGLOVER & FLASH OF STOCKING)

This is a work of fiction. ***All characters are of legal age and are 18 years old or older.***

First Edition. February 2024.

This book was written by and copyright © 2024 Pete Andrews. All rights reserved.

ABOUT THE AUTHOR

I write sexy romances. I used to publish under *xleglover* and *Flash of Stocking* on various sites.

My stories are romances, so they explore the feelings, emotions and relationships of the characters. My stories are also erotica, so the sex scenes are explicit. Often *very* explicit.

My stories have an emotional edge to them. The characters have thrilling adventures, but there's pain there too, at least for some of them.

I try to write stories that seem like real life. Yes, the situations are extreme, but I hope you come away thinking, *"Yes, I can see how that might happened."*

You can find my books wherever e-books are sold. If you'd like to join my mailing list or would like to send me a question or feedback, please email me at *peteandrews1701@gmail.com*.

FORWARD

Before writing as Pete Andrews, I wrote as *xleglover*. Before that, I wrote as *Flash of Stocking*. This is the third collection of stories I published as *xleglover* and *Flash of Stocking*, many years ago. The first collection is called *Wife Watching Game and Other Stories*. The second collection is called *Wife Dates Another Man and Other Stories*. I hope you enjoy this book and check out my other books I've published as Pete Andrews.

LOSING MY WIFE TO ANOTHER MAN

Things didn't look good. I'd lost my job a few months back due to the economy, and I was having the toughest time finding something else. My wife Kaitlin didn't work (she's a stay at home mom with our two kids, a 6 year old boy and a 2 year old girl), and we'd been living on our savings. But those were about gone.

About a month back Kaitlin started looking for a job too. She got good grades in college, but she never worked (we got married right after college, and she got pregnant on our honeymoon). With the rough economy, nobody was hiring a 28-year-old mom with 2 young kids and without any experience.

"You should apply where I work," Rachel said as we sat around our kitchen table sipping wine and trying to figure out what to do. Rachel was Kaitlin's best friend, and she worked in one of the largest advertising firms in the city, Baxter Baxter and Morgan (everyone called it BBM). "Old man Morgan is looking for an executive assistant."

"Do you think he'd hire me?" Kaitlin said hopefully. She shrugged, looking a little defeated. "I mean, I was hoping for something more than being a secretary, but at this point I'll take anything."

Rachel put her hand over Kaitlin's. "Honey, you'd be an executive assistant, not a secretary. With Morgan there's a big difference. You'd have a lot of responsibility, and I hear the pay is really good."

Kaitlin and I both looked at Rachel with interest. This could really help us, tide us over until I got a job. "But do you think he'd hire me?"

"I think you have a good chance. I mean, you majored in marketing and got good grades in college, and you're smart and a hard worker. But there's one thing ...."

"What?" both Kaitlin and I asked almost simultaneously.

"Well, you'd have to work evenings and weekends a lot."

"That's okay," I said. I saw the look in Kaitlin's face and squeezed her hand. "I know it'll be hard being away from the kids, but it'll only be temporary until I get a job."

Rachel held up her hands in warning. "You can't let on to Morgan that it'll only be temporary. He got so mad when his last admin left because he'd just finished training her. She got pregnant and then quit after having the baby."

"Okay, well, I just won't say anything about how long I'll be staying," Kaitlin said shrugging.

"It's more than that," Rachel said. "The rumor is he's only considering single women without kids."

Kaitlin gave her friend a look. "I'm pretty sure that's illegal."

Rachel shrugged. "I know, but what can you do? He's too smart to ever get caught. Anyways, if you want a chance at the job, you'll have to pretend you're single and your career is your life. But the pay is unbelievable. I heard his last admin got almost $300,000 last year."

I looked shocked. That was more than I made in my last job. "You're kidding, how does an admin get paid that much?"

Rachel shrugged again. "Well, like I said, it's a demanding job, you're essentially on call all the time. But you get commissions on the deals old Morgan closes, so the more he makes, the more you make."

⸺⸺◉⸺⸺

A WEEK LATER, I WAITED anxiously for Kaitlin to get home from her interview. If something didn't work out soon, we'd have to sell our house. We needed this job.

"How did it go?" I asked jumping up as soon as she got home. Her face was all smiles.

"I got it!" she squealed. "I start Monday!"

4

We celebrated by taking the kids to their favorite restaurant, McDonalds of course. Fortunate too, since that was about the only restaurant that fit in the current state of our finances.

Then mom and dad did their own celebrating after putting the kids down. "I think I'm going to like this Mister Mom thing," I said nuzzling Kaitlin's neck as she got into bed.

"Oh, really? Well, you know, there's more to staying home than watching ESPN all day," she playfully teased. We both were in great moods because our financial disaster seemed to have been averted.

"I know that," I said with mocked seriousness. "I mean, there's the Golf Channel too. But what I'm really looking forward to is seeing my sexy wife all dressed up for work every day."

"Hmmm, and why is that?" she asked playing dumb. "I won't be wearing anything special. Just short skirts, hose and high heels." She giggled, and then I attacked her.

Kaitlin knew I loved it when she dressed up, but taking care of the kids, she usually just wore t-shirts and baggy sweats, which did a good job of hiding her best features. At 28 and even after 2 kids, my wife still had her youthful good looks. Lush dark hair that went over her shoulders, beautiful face, and a slim figure with medium and beautifully shaped, firm breasts (even after breast feeding our kids). A tight, shapely behind. And long, shapely legs that were her best assets, which suited me just fine because I was a leg man.

The next day I worked on fixing a leaky sink while Kaitlin and Rachel sorted through her closet. "Kaitlin, you're going to have to get some new clothes, this is all so last decade," Rachel said holding up one of Kaitlin's dresses with a clear look of disapproval on her face. "You've got to remember, this is advertising, and you've got to look young and energetic. All of your clothes look like mom clothes."

"What can I say, I'm a mom," Kaitlin said shrugging. She hadn't bought any new clothes in a long time, besides maternity clothes. She even had to borrow an outfit from Rachel for the interview.

Rachel took Kaitlin's face in her hands, looking serious. "Sweetie, you've got to get out of that mindset. If old man Morgan suspects you have kids, or you're married, he'll fire you! And I'll be in trouble too for recommending you!"

"Okay, okay, I get it," Kaitlin said, her hands up in surrender. "But I can't afford to buy new clothes now."

Rachel reached into her bag and pulled out some clothes. "Here, I brought you some outfits to tide you over until your first check. Luckily we're about the same size."

Kaitlin looked doubtfully at her friend, who was busty, Ds to Kaitlin's Cs. "I meant from the waist down," Rachel said laughing.

Kaitlin gave Rachel the evil eye, then sorted through what Rachel had brought. They were all short skirts, none longer than mid-thigh and tailored to hug curves, and a few pairs of high heels. She knew the skirts would be tight, but they'd probably work for now.

"Well, Connor is going to love seeing me in these things," she said with a grin.

"Hey, no funny business while your wife is wearing my clothes," Rachel said my way in a threatening voice, but then gave me a wink. "Or at least, make sure they come back to me dry cleaned."

I gave Rachel a "*who me*?" innocent look, and then laughed.

Then Rachel gave Kaitlin a $200 gift card to Victoria's Secret. "You can pay me back later. You need to get some thongs. I know, I know, you hate them, but panty lines are a major *faux pas*. And buy thigh high stockings too."

Rachel waved her hand dismissively at my wife's "*what the heck*?" look. She said, "It'll make you feel sexy, and you'll need that extra self-confidence when you're dealing with all the male jerks at the office. Trust me on this one. "

I couldn't help smiling. "This is getting better and better," I joked. Then I had to dodge quickly as my wife threw one of the stiletto heels at me.

———◆———

AT FIRST IT WAS ROUGH for Kaitlin. She had to learn a lot at her new job, and she hated being away from the kids. Having me home taking care of them (instead of putting them in daycare) helped a lot. Having to pretend she was single without any kids didn't help, because she couldn't confide in anyone at work except Rachel.

But after a couple of months things got better. She started getting the hang of the job, and it was actually interesting and challenging. And the money was great. With Kaitlin's help, old man Morgan closed a couple of big deals, and we were both wide-eyed at the size of her commissions. We got current with our mortgage, and even started rebuilding some of our savings, and that was *after* buying Kaitlin a new work wardrobe.

I have to admit, that was my favorite part (next to avoiding bankruptcy). Kaitlin learned fast that BBM wasn't one of those business casual places that are so common today. Men and women were expected to dress like they had just stepped out of *GQ* and *Vogue* magazine. Old man Morgan was famous for saying, "If you can't sell yourself, how the fuck are you going to sell our clients?"

I wasn't complaining about Kaitlin's new wardrobe. She came home every day looking hot in her designer dresses and high heels! I liked watching her get dressed – especially since she had taken Rachel's advice about the thong panties and thigh high stockings – and I liked it even better after putting the kids down, when I got my sexy wife into bed. With the stress of our almost financial ruin behind us, we were both less stressed, and our sex life was as good as it'd ever been.

A crowd of the 20- and 30-something BBMers always went out for drinks Friday night, and after making excuses for a few weeks, Kaitlin finally started going. Even though she hated being away from me and the kids for even more time, she didn't have a choice, because she had to keep up the appearance she was an unattached single woman. Usually, she cut out at the earliest opportunity, but one Friday night she didn't get home until past midnight. She was drunk and incredibly horny. She practically raped me as soon as she got home.

The next morning, she was nursing a hangover, and didn't start feeling like herself again until after lunch. I asked what happened last night to get her so worked up, not that I was complaining as our sex had been great.

She hesitantly told me their group started dancing, and some of the men danced really close to her, so there was some bumping and grinding. She looked worried I'd be mad, but I told her I understood. It was just some singles going out after a hard week at work and blowing off steam, and anyways I benefitted from it with having an extremely horny wife in bed. She looked relieved and our weekend continued as normal.

Kaitlin continued going out with her co-workers on Fridays, getting home usually past midnight. She always came home horny, and we had great sex sessions. I could tell she now looked forward to these Friday nights with her co-workers, which kind of bothered me but I didn't say anything because I remembered how I'd often go out with the men for a drink when I was working. Also, our sex after she got home on Fridays was always great. I was getting it more now than ever before. Often we did it with Kaitlin still wearing the thigh high stockings and high heels, and that was mind blowing for me.

Also, I started looking forward to hearing how her male co-workers took liberties with her during these Friday evening happy hours. Kaitlin always told me everything. She has always been an *"honesty is the best policy"* kind of person.

It surprised me that I got turned on by her stories, but looking back I'd always enjoyed seeing other men giving her attention. So, usually when she got home on those Friday nights, we'd rush to bed (the kids would already be asleep). She would always be turned on by all the male attention she'd gotten, and me anxious yet also excited to hear what had happened. We'd get naked (I always made her keep her stockings and high heels on), and then slowly make love as she recounted all the details of that evening.

━━━◉━━━

FALL TURNED INTO WINTER, and BBM's Christmas party was nearing, and Kaitlin was bringing me as her "date" so we both could have fun, as BBM had the reputation of throwing over-the-top lavish parties. From the beginning, we had worked out a good cover story. Kaitlin was a recent divorcee. That explained why she hadn't been working since college. I was her cousin, and she was living with me until she got back on her feet. I had 2 kids, and my wife had passed away a couple of years ago. This was close enough to the truth, so we wouldn't accidentally out ourselves. And by not portraying me as her boyfriend, we didn't have to worry about her boss (Morgan) thinking she was about to get married.

Also, leading up to the Christmas party, our sex was extra fun pretending we were cousins. Kaitlin and I laughed about it, but we both found that "kissing cousins" taboo to be exciting. I guess we both were kind of kinky.

I think she worried about me seeing her with her rowdy male friends. It was one thing to tell me about their shenanigans, and another for me to see it in person. I told her not to worry about it. I didn't think anyone would do anything too wild at a company party. But inside, I secretly hoped some of the men got frisky with her, because (strangely enough) I found the idea arousing.

The evening of the party, I wore my best suit. Kaitlin had bought a new dress, and she looked stunning. It was a designer off-the-shoulder black number that hugged her curves and showed off a lot of her great legs.

We arrived and Kaitlin introduced me to her co-workers. I fetched Kaitlin a drink, and then another one. I was pretending to be a nice-guy cousin, but in fact I wanted to loosen her up so she'd have a good time. We agreed people might get suspicious if we stayed together and looked like a real couple, so at times we drifted apart, talking to different groups of people.

A group of about 30 people seemed to be the center of attention. They looked like a clique, like the popular kids in high school. As I found out, they were the elite group of young executives on the fast track in BBM. It surprised me to see my wife in this group.

In this group were the people she had introduced me too, so clearly this was the Friday night gang. All of them were very good looking and extremely well dressed, like models and movie stars at a Hollywood bash.

My wife fit right in. She looked so beautiful and sexy in her new dress, so confident among all the other beautiful people.

I knew I didn't fit into that crowd, and it bothered me. But seeing her there, clearly the center of attention of a number of the men, I felt a stirring in my loins. Later that night, as we made love, I fantasized about those men having sex with my wife.

The next week I did a lot of thinking. Seeing Kaitlin at the Christmas party among the *Populars* (as I thought of them) brought back college memories. With her good looks and bubbly personality, Kaitlin was extremely popular back in college. I kind of admired her from afar, because there was no way a girl like her was going to go out with a geeky guy like me. But she almost failed a math class, so her teacher assigned me as her tutor (I was a teaching assistant). I think it surprised her as much as me when she fell in love with me, just like it surprised her friends (including her BFF Rachel), and I think her parents too.

The Christmas party disturbed me because my wife was once again hanging around a crowd that I thought we had left behind in college. The crowd of *beautiful people*, the crowd I could never fit into. What disturbed me more were the fantasies growing in my head, of my wife with these handsome and charismatic men. It was all confusing. I didn't tell Kaitlin any of this, as I wanted to work it out for myself first.

A couple of weeks later I came into the kitchen where Kaitlin and Rachel were huddled close together. They were sipping wine and giggling, but when I walked in, they abruptly stopped talking.

"What's up?" I asked.

The girls looked at each other, and Rachel gave Kaitlin a "*you've got to tell him*" look. My wife's eyes shot arrows through her friend, but then she finally said, "Well, one of the men at work asked me out."

"That's not true," Rachel quickly corrected. "Men have been asking you out since you started working at BBM."

I looked inquiring at my wife. "They have? You didn't tell me."

"I'm sorry. I didn't think it was a big thing. I mean, of course I'm not going out with any of them. I'm married for god's sakes."

"And that's my point," Rachel said, looking sagely at both me and Kaitlin. "Kaitlin, people are starting to talk, wondering why you never go out on dates. Pretty soon they're going to suspect you're married, and as soon as that happens old man Morgan is going to can your butt."

The two friends frowned at each other. Clearly this was a conversation they had been having for some time. Even before I said it, I knew I shouldn't. It wasn't wise to listen to your small head instead of your big head.

"Maybe Rachel is right," I said shrugging and pretending to look nonchalant. "I mean, you're making a lot of money at this job, and we don't want to take a chance of people suspecting."

So, that's how my wife started dating other men. At the start it was an extension of her Friday nights out. They'd go out as a group to start the evening, then Kaitlin and her date would go off alone. Instead of getting home around midnight, she started getting home closer to 2am or even later. When she got home, we'd fuck until almost daylight. Thank god her parents lived nearby, as we got into the routine of having the kids sleep over Friday nights so we'd be able to sleep in Saturday morning.

I made Kaitlin tell me everything she did on her dates. She didn't understand my fascination, but was always open with me, I think partly because she always came home at least a little drunk, and also because I think it helped her deal with the guilt of enjoying her nights out so much. The fact I never got mad or upset also helped her be forthcoming (in fact, it was exactly the opposite, her stories turned me on).

Kaitlin always came home hot from her dates, even more so than the Friday night happy hours. As you'd expect, men took more liberties with her when they had her alone on dates. She wouldn't let them get too far, but definitely some kissing and fondling took place. She never let anyone get inside her blouse or up her skirt, but still the increased intimacy always got her soaking wet and me rock hard, and our sex got even more passionate and torrid.

Sometimes her dates were on Saturday nights, and it was weird when her date picked her up at our house. I was pretending to be her cousin, so of course I had to act like everything was normal, just my pretty popular cousin going out on a date. But it was a strange – and stimulating – experience to make small talk with a man who was taking my wife out on a date, and then see my wife walk into the room dressed in one of her sexy clubbing outfits, and see her give her date a hello kiss on the lips.

On her date nights, I spent a lot of time thinking about what my wife was doing with her date. It got me terribly excited imagining them holding hands, his arm around her, kissing, his hand running up her thigh. I usually masturbated once or twice while waiting, and my arousal was so great I still had enough in the tank to fuck her when she got home.

I discovered I wasn't alone in my fantasy to see my wife with other men. I found websites like *literotica.com* and *ourhotwives.org* (and the list of e-books on *Kindle* were endless), and the posts and stories helped me better understand myself, although they didn't help with my doubts and insecurities with being complicit with my wife seeing other men.

After a few months of dating, Kaitlin had progressed to heavy kissing and petting. Her date often invited her up to his apartment, but so far she hadn't done that, so mostly they fooled around in darken corners of a club, or in the guy's car. She was letting men inside her blouse and bra, and even up her skirt. She said men went crazy when they discovered she was wearing real stockings. She said her date often audibly moaned when his hand passed from her stocking top to her bare thigh above, realizing she was wearing thigh highs and not pantyhose.

She told me it was hard to hold off men to just petting over clothes especially when it was their third or fourth date. Thus, we agreed she'd go on no more than five dates with the same man. She was fine with this as it wasn't like she was looking for a serious relationship (since of course she had me), and I liked it because it was dangerous enough to make it really exciting.

We developed some other rules to make sure Kaitlin's dating didn't hurt our marriage. Mouth kissing was okay, as was petting over and under clothes. But undressing wasn't allowed. She was allowed to let a man unbutton her blouse and even unsnap her bra, but she couldn't let him take clothes completely off her. Her date could finger her and even make her cum, but that was it, no oral and certainly no intercourse. Likewise, she was allowed to touch him anywhere including giving him a hand job, but no oral. Her mouth (and of course her pussy) were off limited.

We decided on these rules gradually, usually as we fucked after one of her dates. "Do you think I went too far?" she would ask huskily after describing something she'd done, or let her date do to her. I'd respond between gasps with, "No, that was okay," or maybe "Yeah, that was okay, you could even have let him do more, like ...."

ONE FRIDAY NIGHT, KAITLIN got home from a date with tears streaked down her face. She fell into my arms sobbing, crying "I'm sorry, I'm sorry," over and over again. She had broken (shattered really) our most important rule. She'd let her date fuck her.

It started with breaking the no oral rule. She'd gotten hot and heavy with Darren, a really *tall-dark-and-handsome* hunky guy (as she described him) she'd been out with a couple of times before. They were necking pretty heavily, and his hands were inside her blouse and bra.

Darren was really good at alternating between softly kneading her breasts, rolling her nipples between his thumb and forefinger, and licking her. Soon she was writhing under his mouth and fingers, so she didn't resist when he moved a hand up her skirt.

Kaitlin gasped when Darren reached her soaking panties, and he was just as good with fingering her clit as he was with stimulating her nipples, so she didn't stop him when he pushed her skirt up around her waist and eased her legs apart. She was in nirvana as he sucked her nipples and fingered her clit, feeling an orgasm build inside her.

Kaitlin knew she was about to break a rule when Darren got on his knees between her legs and his face moved towards her pussy, but she figured she'd cum with his first lick on her clit, so it wouldn't be too much of a rule violation. She even raised up her hips when he pulled off her thong panties.

But she underestimated how good Darren was at eating pussy, and he kept her on the edge of an orgasm for what seemed like an eternity, until she practically begged him to let her cum.

It was then, when she was most vulnerable, that Darren struck. Unbeknownst to her, while eating her out, he had pulled his cock from his pants. Before she knew what was happening, he raised up from his knees and pushed his cock into her soaking pussy.

This wasn't rape. True, she pushed against his chest as soon as he penetrated her, and said *no* a couple of times, but she was so far gone by that point, and his cock felt so good inside her, that soon she was pushing against his thrusts, urging him to fuck her harder, throwing her arms around his neck and pulling his face to hers so she could kiss him as he had his way with her.

Kaitlin cried uncontrollably as she told me what had happened. It was more than just breaking the rules and letting another man fuck her. She had gotten so caught up in it that she hadn't made him pull out, so he had cum inside her. This was bad because she wasn't on the pill – I'd had a vasectomy after our second child—and it was her fertile time of the month.

I took her into my arms and comforted her. "It's not your fault, this was bound to happen sooner or later," I said softly as I gently kissed her tears away.

Then I laid her on her back and pushed up her skirt. She hadn't bothered to put her panties back on, and her trimmed bush was matted with Darren's cum. I took out my cock and entered my wife. She welcomed me inside her, as confirmation I wasn't mad, that I still loved her.

I'd never been as excited in my life, and I fucked her harder than ever before. After just moments, I grunted and lurched, and added my sperm to Darren's already inside her. The only difference was, my sperm was blanks and his was live bullets.

The next day, we went to the drug store and got a morning after pill. She took it and then cried some more, and we made love again. Like before, she welcomed me between her legs, reaffirming our commitment to each other and our marriage.

Over the next week, we had sex more than ever before. The image of Darren fucking Kaitlin kept me perpetually hard, and after what had happened, Kaitlin wasn't denying me anything.

A few days after her date with Darren she was finally able to talk more about it, and I littered her with questions, wanting to know every detail. Yes, he had a nice muscular body. Yes, he was bigger, a little longer, and thicker. Yes, he had made her cum.

For a few weeks after, she didn't go out on any dates. She didn't even go to the Friday night happy hours.

Darren called repeatedly. He was worried she was mad at him. He was a nice guy and hadn't done anything wrong, so Kaitlin finally decided to go out with him again.

The week leading up to her date was kind of awkward for us. What were the rules now?

I decided to make things easy for both of us. As she prepared to go, I handed her a bag from the drug store. Kaitlin looked inquiring at me, then looked in the bag, where she saw a box of condoms.

I took my wife into my arms and looked into her beautiful eyes. "Just don't fall in love with anyone else," I told her. She nodded, understanding.

Now we had just one rule. *Don't fall in love.*

"Of course I won't," Kaitlin promised. Then she pulled me into our bed and we made love, just minutes before Darren was to arrive to pick her up. I came inside her just as the doorbell rang.

I went downstairs to greet Darren as she put herself back together for her date. They left holding hands, but then I heard Kaitlin say, "Wait, I forgot something."

She came back inside and, with the half open door blocking Darren's view, she hitched up her skirt and pulled my hand to her lacy stocking top. It was moist. "You're running out of me," she whispered with a mischievous smile and twinkle in her eye. Then she ran back out and took Darren's arm for her date.

SOMETIMES I MET KAITLIN and her friends at their Friday night happy hours. It was a little awkward, because I didn't fit in, but Kaitlin's friends put up with me because I was her cousin. Kaitlin got over her nervousness of having me around, sometimes playfully winking at me or pinching my butt when no one was looking.

Typically, Kaitlin stayed with the group until 9pm or so, and then left with her date. She had a date almost every weekend. She was a very popular girl at work. Rachel sometimes complained (playfully) that Kaitlin had more dates than her.

It was excruciatingly delicious to watch Kaitlin disappear with her date, holding his hand. Kaitlin usually had sex on her dates. From that first time with Darren, sex went from sometimes, to often, to just about on every date.

She didn't need to tell me when she had sex. I knew as soon as she got home just by looking at her. She'd have that *"just fucked"* look. Sex with her then was amazing, smelling her date in her hair, seeing his marks on her neck and breasts, feeling her looser than normal pussy.

Sometimes we'd be with friends the day after one of her dates, and someone would comment on a hickey on her neck. "Jeez guys, what are you, still newlyweds?" We'd laugh with everyone else, but Kaitlin would nudge me under the table, reminding me another man had put that mark on her, not me. She teased me like that because I loved it, and *she knew* I loved it.

Sex was a no-commitment recreation sport among the Populars. They were all *"career comes first"* kind of people, and weren't interested in serious relationships. So, Kaitlin's sleeping around didn't hurt her reputation, because *everyone* was sleeping around. If anything, her popularity increased once it got around how hot a body she had and how great a lover she was.

For the longest time, I practically begged Kaitlin to let me watch her have sex with another man. She always found a reason not to, explaining she wasn't ready for that.

We were at a party thrown by one of the BBM partners about six months after her first time with Darren. We were pretending to be "cousins" again. I hadn't seen Kaitlin for about an hour when I felt a hand on my shoulder. "Be in the master bedroom in five minutes," I heard my wife whisper in my ear.

My cock immediately got hard. I quickly snuck into the bedroom, and hid in the closet, leaving the door open so I had a clear view of the bed. A few minutes later Kaitlin entered followed closely by a man.

To my surprise, it wasn't her date Darren, but the BBM partner who was hosting the party. I had met him earlier, his name was Ekon. Maybe early thirties, standing a head taller than my wife's 5'3". He'd probably be described as ruggedly handsome. He seemed to be an okay guy when I met him.

Most importantly though, he was black. *Black!* I later found out his parents immigrated to the US from Nigeria. Ekon was born here in the states.

"I've noticed you. Heard a lot about you," Ekon said pulling my wife into his arms. "They say you've got a tight body."

"Are they right?" my wife gasped as Ekon ran his hands over her body.

"We'll see," Ekon said with a grin, unzipping her dress so it fell off her body and puddled around her high heeled feet. He looked her up and down and smiled. Kaitlin had gone braless, wearing only stockings, a lacy garter belt, thong panties, and high heels. "Nice," he said, cupping her tits. "I've wanted you for a long time."

My wife's breasts were medium size – Cs – and still ripe and perfect, even at 28 years old, even after giving birth to two babies and breastfeeding both. They were firm and shapely and perky with slightly upturned eraser-sized nipples.

Kaitlin's eyes glazed over as Ekon expertly rolled her nipples between his thumbs and forefingers. "You like that Kaitlin?"

"Yeah," she breathed huskily. Her breast and nipples had always been extremely sensitive. If anything after breastfeeding, they were more sensitive now than before.

She gasped as one of his hands went down to her pussy.

"Are you serious with Darren? I see you with him a lot."

Kaitlin shook her head, her brunette locks swaying side to side. "We're just friends," she said distractedly, her eyes closed as her whole being seemed focused on what his fingers were doing to her body. "You've noticed me?" she asked, referring to what he said a moment before.

"I've admired you from afar," he said kissing her neck, his fingers continuing to work on her nipples and clit.

"You've got me so hot," Ekon said, moving his hands from her body long enough to take off his expensive Italian suit. He had a lean muscular body with a well-defined chest and 6-pack abs, and the biggest cock I'd ever seen. It was jet black like the rest of him.

Kaitlin noticed the size of his cock too, and her eyes grew wide. "Wow, that's big," she said, and then she giggled as she realized how ridiculous she sounded. "Sorry, dizzy girl moment."

Ekon laughed, and then laid her on the bed and got on top of her. His kissed her, softly on her lips, then gently extending his tongue into her mouth. "God you're beautiful," he said looking into her eyes and running his fingers through her lush dark hair, and then they French kissed again. Ekon moved his body so his cock head touched her pussy lips. He saw the worry in Kaitlin's face and kissed her lightly on the lips. "Don't worry, I'll go slow," he said.

"My purse – I have condoms," Kaitlin said.

Ekon looked disappointed, but he reached into her purse and rolled a condom around his cock.

I sat in the closet with my hand around my hard cock. I couldn't believe it, I was about to see another man fuck my wife. And not just any man. A black man!

"Oh god," Kaitlin gasped as Ekon entered her.

"It's okay, I'll go slow," Ekon assured her, kissing her lips and cheeks and stoking her hair. "Just a little bit, now, a little more." Kaitlin gritted her teeth as he slowly pushed more inside her, but she didn't tell him to stop.

"It's all in," Ekon finally said. "Are you okay?"

"Yes, yes, I'm fine," Kaitlin said, her words coming out fast in a manic way. She was breathing hard, and her pretty face was strained with concentration. "It's a lot. You're big. But it feels good. I'm getting used to it."

Ekon smiled, delighted by the compliment of his large manhood. He started moving in and out, slowly at first, and then faster, but not too hard. He was still being gentle.

It took a while for Kaitlin to get used to his size, but eventually her body moved with his. Her long shapely legs flexed with each thrust, the garter straps pressing into her firm thighs, her feet arching out of her heels to push up on her tiptoes to meet his thrusts.

"Oh god, I'm cumming!" Kaitlin cried, her fingers clutching the sheets, and then wrapping around Ekon's neck. Ekon lowered his head and pressed his lips over Kaitlin's, kissing her through her orgasm.

"Oh god, oh god," Kaitlin panted as her orgasm subsided.

Ekon, his hard cock still fully inside her, kissed her softly on the lips and cheek. "Are you okay?" he asked.

"Am I okay?" Kaitlin said with a delighted laugh. "I'm more than okay, that was so good!" She ran her manicured nails over Ekon's muscular chest. "You haven't cum yet. Do you want to stay like this, or me on top? Or something else?"

I grew alarmed. Had my wife just offered her ass to this man? His big cock would tear her apart! But then Kaitlin took Ekon's hand and sensually sucked two of his black fingers into her mouth.

"Do you want this?" Kaitlin said sensually looking into Ekon's eyes.

"That's tempting," Ekon said breathing hard as he watched my wife suck his fingers into her mouth, and felt her soft tongue roll around his fingers. "But this way is good. You feel incredible. I wish I didn't have to wear a condom, though. I hate them. Are you sure I need to wear it? I promise I'm clean."

"I'm sorry, I can't," Kaitlin said, running her hand across Ekon's cheek to soften her refusal. "I trust you, I do. But I'm not on the pill. I'm allergic to it."

That was true. The pill always gave Kaitlin terrible headaches. That was why I got a vasectomy when we decided our family was complete after our second child.

"Oh, okay, I understand then," Ekon said, disappointment still clear on his face.

Kaitlin hesitated, then said, "I guess you can take it off, if you promise to pull out."

"Really?" Ekon said eagerly.

"Really," Kaitlin said kissing him softly on the lips.

"Thank you," Ekon said as he pulled out, reached between their bodies to pull off the condom. He tossed the condom on the floor, and then pushed his cock in again. "God, thank you, this feels so much better."

"It feels better for me too," Kaitlin agreed.

I watched this with growing concern, my eyes lingering on the condom on the floor. Why did Kaitlin agree to no condom? Even if Ekon pulled out, a girl could get pregnant from pre-cum. Kaitlin knew that. And Ekon was black! It wasn't like we could pretend the baby was mine if she got pregnant and we decided to have the baby.

Kaitlin and I were both pro-life. We understood the point of view of pro-choice people, we just happened to be pro-life. If Kaitlin got pregnant, it wasn't like we could run down to the local abortion clinic. There were deep rooted moral issues for us when it came to pregnancy.

I forced myself to calm down. Kaitlin knew what she was doing. Probably, she knew this wasn't her fertile time.

Ekon started fucking Kaitlin again, starting slow and then moving faster. He took long, deep strokes. He put Kaitlin's legs on his shoulders so he could get even deeper, smashing her legs against her tits. Kaitlin grunted and grimaced with this position, as she wasn't used to getting penetrated so deeply, but then got used to it and again began meeting his thrusts.

Ekon had amazing stamina. After fucking Kaitlin missionary for about 10 minutes, he flipped her around onto her stomach and then took her doggy style. As he positioned himself to enter my wife again, I had my first good look at Ekon's cock. It was a very impressive sight, long and thick, with wide veins running up both sides. He was much bigger than me, but the size difference only increased my arousal, as my fantasies always involved Kaitlin getting fucked by well hung men.

And Ekon's cock was black of course, just like the rest of him. As far as I knew, Kaitlin had never dated a black man, either before we met or since she started working at BBM. Did she have secret fantasies about black men? I had to admit, I found the taboo of my lily-white wife with the jet black Ekon very arousing.

Kaitlin gripped the mattress for dear life as Ekon's hard thrusts practically slammed her head into the wall. "Oh god, you're fucking me so hard!" Kaitlin gasped.

Ekon grabbed Kaitlin's hair and jerked her head back. "You like getting it hard?" he growled. He had a long tongue, and he slithered it inside Kaitlin's ear.

"Oh god, oh god," she whimpered at the sensation. I saw Kaitlin's body tense, and I knew she was about to cum again, which surprised me since she'd never been multi-orgasmic.

Ekon sensed it too. He pounded her even harder (if that was possible). He again pulled her head back and French kissed her, while with his other hand he roughly squeezed her nipples from underneath. Kaitlin's moans were lost in Ekon's mouth as her body shuddered in another orgasm.

Ekon timed it perfectly, because his body tensed like he was about to cum at the same time as Kaitlin. Through some amazing self-control, at the last moment the black man pulled out and shot gobs and gobs of thick creamy sperm all over her back.

They collapsed onto the bed, Ekon rolling to his side so they snuggled face to face. They panted into each other's face, gasping for breath, and then their gasps turned into light kissing. I thought they might go at it again, but then Kaitlin softly said, "We better get back." She went into the bathroom to clean up, and when she returned a few minutes later she wiggled back into her black dress. "Can you zip me?" she said turning her back to him. He kissed her on the neck as he zipped her.

"Can I see you again?" Ekon asked.

She giggled like a young schoolgirl. "You see me every day at work," she said.

"You know what I mean," Ekon said grinning.

Ekon had gotten dressed too. With a playful eye, Kaitlin reached into his pocket, and was rewarded by a lustful smile from Ekon.

"Down cowboy, I told you we have to get back," she said playfully, nudging him in the ribs. She pulled his cell phone from his pocket. "Here, I'll put my number into your phone."

After handing the phone back to Ekon, they moved to leave, but Kaitlin held back. "I forgot my purse," she said. She stepped back into the bedroom and grabbed her purse. Just before leaving the room, she looked at the closet and whispered with a twinkle in her eye, "I hope you liked that!"

⎯⎯●⎯⎯

LATER THAT NIGHT, I lay on top of my wife, her legs around me, my cock hard but not yet inside her.

"It was incredible, watching you have sex with another man," I told Kaitlin as I looked down into her beautiful face. "It was hot. But – it kind of surprised me too. Sometimes it looked like you were making love, not just fucking. It seemed so –."

I hesitated, struggling to think of the right word.

"Tender," I finally said. "Tender. And loving."

Kaitlin reached up and stroked my cheek reassuringly. "Don't worry honey. Sometimes it's like that. Mostly it's just fucking. But we're people too, so sometimes it's like that." She reached up to kiss me on the lips. "Don't worry honey. You're the only man I love."

"Forever?" I asked, knowing I probably sounded like an insecure kid, not her husband of many years and father of her children, but at that moment I needed her reassurance.

"Forever," she assured me. She pulled me to her. "Make love to me. Now, Connor. I need you inside me."

I didn't need to be asked twice. I excitedly entered her bareback, relishing the feeling of skin on skin. I never wore a condom with Kaitlin, of course, since I was fixed.

"You let Ekon inside you without a condom," I said as I began moving in and out of her.

"I know. It was stupid," Kaitlin admitted. "This is my safe time of the month, but you never know. And I know pre-cum can make you pregnant. I won't do it again."

Kaitlin's admission made me feel better. But I still didn't understand. "Why'd you let him?" I asked,

"I don't know," she said. "It was the heat of the moment I guess."

Kaitlin's explanation didn't comfort me. Heat of the moment? Wasn't fucking, by definition, always "heat of the moment?" So, I still didn't understand why she let Ekon inside her without a condom. But I let it go because her pussy felt so good. It was looser after being with Ekon, but that only make it more exciting. I kissed and fondled my wife as we made passionate love.

After cumming, we lay snuggled facing each other. "Who is he, Ekon? I don't think I've seen him before."

"He's not part of our group. What do you call us, the Populars?" Kaitlin giggled. "Well, he's not part of the Populars. He's a partner, so he's what we're trying to be."

"He seems young to be a partner. His house is amazing."

"I know, right? And they say he has a bigger place in South Beach. He's the youngest person ever to make partner at BBM.

"So ... a black man? I never knew you were into that," I said.

Kaitlin didn't answer. I soon heard her deep and regular breathing. Exhausted, she'd fallen asleep.

⟢⟁⟢

THE NEXT DAY, I FOUND Kaitlin and Rachel giggling in our kitchen. Rachel, of course, knew all about Kaitlin's dates and the sex she had with the men at BBM. There were no secrets between the BFFs. Rachel also knew I got off on my wife's adventures with other men. I wasn't sure how I felt about Rachel knowing, but she had never made fun of me. If anything, I think she admired me for being so open-minded and giving Kaitlin some freedom to explore her wild side.

Rachel *certainly* had a wide side. Like Kaitlin, she was young, pretty and sexy, and a committed single. She vowed to never get married as she couldn't imagine having sex with the same man for the rest of her life.

Rachel looked up at me as I approach. With both a laugh and admiration in her voice (and maybe some envy too), she said, "I can't believe Kaitlin hooked Desirable #1."

I smiled at the *Harry Potter* reference, the opposite of *Undesirable*. "You mean Ekon?" I asked.

"*Yes*, I'm talking about Ekon!" Rachel said enthusiastically. "I'd been trying to catch his eye forever! Hunky and rich, what a combination! Everyone's talking about it! God Kaitlin! I can't believe you went as Darren's date but then fucked Ekon! What a heartless slut!"

Kaitlin kicked her friend under the table. "Shush," she cautioned looking around. "The kids might hear."

Rachel covered her mouth with an apologetic "*oops*" look, and then the conversation went to other things.

A COUPLE WEEKS LATER, Kaitlin plopped on the sofa next to me, looking thoughtful. "I'm thinking about going out with Ekon," she said. "He's been asking me out. I want to make sure you're okay with that. I won't if you don't want me too." Then she smiled impishly. "Honestly, the biggest reason I want to go out with him is to make Rachel and the other Populars jealous."

I felt my cock stir. "It's fine with me," I said. With a laugh, I said, "After all, he's Desirable #1. What does that mean, anyways?"

Kaitlin giggled. "It means he's a man you'd give up your other fuck buddies for." She straddled my lap and wrapped her arms around my neck, running her fingers through my hair. "Of course, you're so kinky I get to be married to you a wonderful *and* have my fuck buddies."

I ran my hands up my wife's blouse and cupped her perfect, braless tits (she often went braless at home). "Is that what you're going to do, add Ekon to your harem of fuck buddies?"

"My harem, I like that. *Mmmm*, yeah, I like *that*," she cooed as I rubbed her nipples between my thumbs and forefingers. "Yeah, I think I *will* add him to my harem. He has a really big one, you know."

"And he's black," I pointed out.

"Oh, you noticed?" Kaitlin teased with a grin. "What do you think about that? Your sweet wife with a black man?"

"I never knew you had a thing for black men," I said.

"It's not a *thing*," Kaitlin said with a laugh. "But everyone knows about the taboo. White girl with a black man. And their reputation for having really big ones."

"It's not just reputation with Ekon," I pointed out.

"I know, right?" Kaitlin said with another laugh. "That man is seriously big."

"Should I be worried?" I teased. "Are you becoming a size queen?"

"A size queen for big black cocks?" Kaitlin joked back. "Don't worry honey. Size isn't the most important thing. Knowing what to do with it, that matters most. And you're the best."

"You *do* like big though," I said. I knew all the men she had been with at BBM were bigger than me. It was part of our pillow talk after her dates.

I pulled my hard cock out of my pants and pushed her skirt up around her waist (thank goodness the kids were already asleep!). I reached up, tugged her panties to the side, and pushed my cock into her. "Are you a slut for big cocks now?"

"Yeah, I'm a slut," Kaitlin breathed hotly into my ear as she began moving up and down on my shaft. "But you like that, don't you cowboy? You *want* your wife to be a slut."

My cock twitched when she called me *cowboy*, remembering she'd called Ekon the same thing. Kaitlin noticed my excitement, and also remembered she'd called Ekon that.

"I called Ekon that because he wore a silly cowboy costume at last year's Halloween party," she explained answering my silent question. Then she looked at me with an inquisitive grin. "You *like* the idea of me dating Ekon, don't you?"

"Yes, I do. I'm not sure why," I admitted. "He seems -—dangerous."

"Dangerous," Kaitlin repeated, as if contemplating the word. Then she leaned closer to me and whispered hotly in my ear. "That's good, because, you know, slutty girls like dangerous boys."

"Maybe he's dangerous because he's black," I said.

"Maybe," Kaitlin agreed with a sly smile on her beautiful face.

"Is that why you let Ekon inside you without a condom?" I asked. "Because he's black?"

"I don't know about that," Kaitlin said with a laugh. I was still inside her, and she was slowly moving up and down. "I told you, it was the heat of the moment."

"Maybe you didn't make him use a condom because you wanted him to like you," I said. "He *is* Desirable #1."

"A girl has to do what a girl has to do," Kaitlin said.

"Are you serious?" I asked.

"Honey, I'm teasing," Kaitlin said. She kissed me, and we continued to make love.

———◉———

A FEW MONTHS LATER

———◉———

IN THE YEAR KAITLIN had been dating and having sex with men at BBM, she typically had her regulars (what I called them), a group of men she regularly dated and fucked. A few like Darren were always on the list, but others rotated on and off. It was like that with all the Populars. Everyone had their regular fuck buddies.

"Who are you going out with tonight?" I asked as Kaitlin pulled on her stockings, getting ready for work. I loved watching her get dressed, and I did it every morning as I was still a stay-at-home dad. She'd shower, rub moisturizer over her entire body, then put on her bra, panties and stockings (and garter belt, when she wore one; otherwise, thigh highs). Then she'd do her hair and makeup, wiggle into her dress or blouse and skirt, and finally slip into her high heels.

"Ekon," she said matter-of-factly. "Can you zip me?" she asked turning her back to me and holding her long brunette hair to the side. Recently she added reddish highlights to her lush brunette hair, so now she looked even more like a model or movie starlet.

"Again? You've been seeing a lot of him."

She shook out her hair and turned to look at me. "You don't want me to go out with him? If you don't, I won't."

"No, it's not that. I'm just curious why you don't go out with the Populars as much anymore."

"I don't know. I still go to the Friday happy hours, but ... I don't know. I guess it's nice to go out with someone who actually likes to talk before fucking me. I mean, basically, Darren and the other Popular boys see me as just a pretty chick with nice tits and long legs. With Ekon, at least he takes me to dinner or a show before getting into my pants."

"Dinner and shows – definitely sounds like more than fucking," I said feeling chagrined.

"That's why it's called a date," Kaitlin said giving me a quick kiss on the lips. "I've really got to go, I'm late. Honey, tell me the truth, does it bother you I'm dating Ekon? Because if it does, I'll stop."

"No, it doesn't bother me, it's just ... no, it doesn't bother me."

Kaitlin looked at me, giving me an inquisitive look as if trying to read my mind, then a curious smile. "I've really got to go," she said hurriedly. "See you late tonight." And with another quick kiss she was gone.

⸺◉⸺

OVER THE NEXT FEW MONTHS, Kaitlin went from dating Ekon sometimes, to mostly, and then exclusively. She hardly went to the happy hours anymore, instead starting her date with Ekon immediately after work on Friday. More and more, she'd go out with Ekon both Friday *and* Saturday nights, staying out late and getting home very freshly fucked. It was annoying me, and the breaking point was when he texted her on Christmas eve. We were at church with our kids when his text came in.

"Oh no," she said. "It's Ekon. He just found out his mother died."

We argued on the way home, and then carried our argument into the privacy of our bedroom away from the kids' ears. "So, you've leaving, on Christmas eve?"

"Connor, honey, his mother just died, and he's all broken up," she said slipping out of her flats and taking off her dress and pantyhose. "I have to go."

"No, you don't have to go. You should stay with me and our children. It's Christmas eve."

"Honey, the kids are already asleep," she said. It was 9pm. She rolled stockings up her legs and attached them to a garter belt. Then she shimmied into skinny jeans. She sat on the bed and slipped into *Jimmy Choo* stiletto ankle boots, her long, lush dark hair almost touching the floor as she leaned over and zipped them.

"I won't be gone too long," she said, taking off her bra and then pulling on a silky white, body-hugging cashmere sweater. "I'll be back later tonight," she promised, adding with a smile to ease the tension, "even before Santa gets here." She brushed her hair swiftly and painted on brownish-red lipstick.

"If you're just going to see if he's okay, then why are you getting all dressed up?" I challenged her.

I guess my angry tone finally got to her, and she lost her patience. She said in an impatient, harsh tone, "So, what Connor, are you going to start dressing me now? I'm just trying to be comfortable, that's all."

"Comfortable? That's a joke. Those jeans are so tight I can see the bumps of your garter belt. And what's up with wearing a garter belt and stockings under jeans? And I noticed you took off your bra. I can see your nipples right through your sweater. You never dress like this for me. My god Kaitlin, you look like a slut!"

Kaitlin glared at me, and then looked away, hurt coming over her beautiful face. "You know, you've called me that before, but this is the first time I think you mean it." A tear came to her eye, and she wiped it away. "I'm a different person with Ekon. This is how I dress when I'm with him. I can't dress this way at church. I know it's Christmas eve. I want to be here with you. But I'm friends with Ekon. It'd be the same way with Rachel if she just found out her mother died. I'll go there, make sure he's okay, and then get back as fast as I can."

"Then why did you put stockings on? Why did you take your bra off?"

"I don't know Connor! I just told you! This is how I dress when I see him! I wasn't even thinking!" she said frustrated. She was quiet for a few moments, like she was counting to 10 to calm down. In a more calm, reasonable voice, she said, "If you're worried I'm going over there to fuck him, I'm not. I just want to make sure he's okay."

"That's what really bothers me," I said with a frown at her. "This thing you have with Ekon. It's not just physical, it's emotional. Remember your promise? You promised never to fall in love with anyone."

Kaitlin took my face gently into her hands. She said, "Let's talk about this later, okay? I promise I won't be gone for long."

We eyed each other silently for long moments, then I finally nodded my head. She kissed me.

"I love you Connor, I really do," Kaitlin said. "I won't be gone long. I promise."

⎯⎯⎯◉⎯⎯⎯

KAITLIN DIDN'T GET back until after 3am. I lay in bed awake, pretending to read a magazine. One look at her told me immediately he'd fucked her, and the guilt on her face confirmed it. She sat on edge of the bed next to me and started to apologize, but I brushed her away. She looked about to cry, and long silent moments passed between us.

Then she leaned into me. That's what she usually did after getting back from a date. She'd lean into me and kiss me so I could taste him in her mouth, smell him in her hair, in her clothes, on her body.

She did that now. I tried to pull away, but she knew me too well. She straddled my stomach and pulled her sweater off, showing the bite marks he'd left on her tits, around her nipples. She pressed her bosom against my face, holding my head tight and feeding her nipples into my mouth.

She kicked off her ankle boots – I heard them fall on the floor – and then wiggled out of her tight jeans. Her panties were gone, but she still wore the garter belt and stockings (I saw her stockings were heavily laddered, no doubt from the hard fucking he'd given her). She reached between our bodies and guided my cock into her pussy. She felt incredibly loose and wet.

I knew where that wetness came from.

"You let him cum inside you, didn't you?" I challenged her.

She answered my question with a question. "Are you still mad at me?"

"Answer my question!" I demanded.

"Tell me you're not mad at me anymore, and I'll tell you."

"Damn it Kaitlin, it doesn't work that way! *DID YOU LET HIM CUM IN YOU*?" I demanded again.

Kaitlin hesitated, like she was giving me time to calm down. Then she said, "I felt so bad for him. He was really close to his mom, and his father died 3 years ago. He doesn't have any brothers or sisters. So, he's all alone now."

"So, you *did* let him cum inside you!" I angrily hissed at her.

"Connor, honey, did you just hear what I said?" Kaitlin asked, trying to reason with me.

"Kaitlin, he's black! And you're not on the pill!"

"I'm safe now."

"No girl is ever 100% safe! You know that! What's wrong with you? What if he gets you pregnant? A half-black baby! What will our parents say? Our kids? Our friends?"

Finally, my words got through to her. All the guilt and misgivings she'd been forcing herself not to think about burst to the surface and she began to cry.

"I don't know what to do, Connor," Kaitlin said helplessly as tears flowed down her face. "I can't resist him. I can't."

My anger faded from me, replaced by numbness, and dread. "Do you love with him?" I asked.

"I'm sorry!" she said as she hugged me and cried into my chest. "I'm so sorry!"

———◉———

KAITLIN STOPPED SEEING Ekon, at least socially (she still saw him at work of course). It was hard for her. She didn't bring him up, but I could tell she was heartbroken.

When she told him – I guess you'd say when she broke up with him – she revealed she was married to me, that I wasn't her cousin, that this ruse wasn't meant to hurt anyone, just to help her get a job (I agreed she had to come clean with him).

Ekon was devastated. He'd fallen in love with Kaitlin. He got so emotional he threatened to tell Morgan and get Kaitlin fired. But in the end, he kept Kaitlin's secret. What can I say? Ekon was a decent man, which was bad in a way, because it was impossible for me to hate him.

Kaitlin stopped going to the Friday happy hours. Everyone assumed she was heartbroken over her breakup with Ekon, and I knew they were right.

Kaitlin never used the L word about Ekon, but we both knew. Her despair over another man, that she'd *fallen in love* with another man, ate away at me, ate away at our relationship, ate away at our marriage. We took care of the kids, but otherwise sleepwalked through life. Our sex life became nonexistent. We tried marriage counseling, but that didn't help, and we never went back after a couple of times. We both were miserable.

So, I did the only thing I could think of. I told her it would be okay with me if she started seeing Ekon again. What else could I do? We were both miserable, and something had to change.

Kaitlin looked at me like I was crazy. "That's how we got into his," she protested. And she was right. How do you solve a problem, by repeating the same mistakes?

We spent countless nights talking about it. Our sex life returned. It was impossible for me to talk about Kaitlin being with another man and not get aroused, even though it pained my heart. I hated myself for this, and during our talks Kaitlin recognized my self-torment, she saw the tears in my eyes while at the same time my cock was hard. She cried too, because of her heartbreak over Ekon, her guilt over what she was doing to me, and as we cried and held each other, we made love.

Finally, after weeks of talking and agonizing, she approached Ekon. I don't know everything they said. But the main part was whether Ekon could be in a relationship with her, knowing she was married to another man.

Ekon resisted at first. I mean, why would a handsome, successful man, the Desirable #1, settle for that? But eventually he agreed. He wasn't able to resist Kaitlin's beautiful face, her bubbly personality, her perfect breasts, her shapely ass and flat stomach, her long wonderful legs.

Most of all, he loved her.

They fucked that night. I knew it as soon as she got home, even before I tasted him in her mouth, smelled him in her hair, saw the bite marks, felt her loose pussy. Just by looking at her face, I knew.

A little later that night, as we made love, she looked into my eyes and promised, "I'll always love you." I knew she meant it. But I also knew she loved another man too. And it tore me to pieces.

It happened gradually. I think Kaitlin went slow to make sure I was okay with it. But eventually things heated up again between her and Ekon. Like before, they went out on Fridays and Saturdays, and often they snuck away for a quickie at lunch during the week. It was like watching a train wreck happening, at least a train wreck for me.

Their relationship blossomed, even more than before. Sometimes I'd catch Kaitlin giddy while doing normal things like folding the laundry or washing the dishes, or giggling on the phone with Rachel. I knew it was about Ekon. Then she'd see me, and get all serious, worried I'd be upset if she showed joy in her relationship with Ekon.

Kaitlin did as much as she could for me. Our sex was passionate again and we made love almost every day. She'd return home from a date with Ekon and come to me as before, letting me smell him on her, guiding me to her legs where his rough fucking had laddered her stockings, inviting me into her pussy so I could see how loose she was. She knew her relationship with Ekon got me hot, so she never denied me after her dates and answered all my lustful questions. But she also knew her relationship with Ekon broke my heart, so after we made love, she always hugged and kissed me and told me how much she loved me.

———◆———

A COUPLE OF MONTHS after going with Ekon again, we sat on the sofa after putting the kids down for the evening. "Can I ask you something?" Kaitlin began cautiously. "I won't if you don't want me to, but – well, Ekon asked me to stay over on Friday."

"Stay over on Friday," I repeated dumbly. "Stay over at his place, with him?"

"Yeah, I mean – well, yeah," she said, I guess not understanding why I couldn't grasp this simple concept. "I'd be home Saturday morning before the kids got home from my parents, so they wouldn't even know I was gone."

But *I'd* know, I thought. I'd be alone, while you let him fuck you all night long, and then you'll sleep with him, and wake up in his arms, and then you'll let him fuck you again before coming home. I thought these things but didn't say them to her.

"I won't if you don't want me to," she repeated seeing my hesitation, but I could tell she wanted to.

I forced a smile. "Sure, that's okay with me, no problem."

Kaitlin smiled back, and then she did what she always did, she sealed the deal with her body, which she knew I couldn't resist. She wasn't being manipulative. For her, it was emotional as much as physical. It was confirmation we were okay. My cock hard inside her, my orgasm, meant I was okay. I was fine with it. Our marriage was good.

Of course, it didn't really work that way. But it eased her guilt at least temporarily, and I'd never pass up a chance to kiss her pretty face, fondle her breasts, feel her long legs around me, be inside her pussy.

Of course, it wasn't just *one* Friday night. It became *most* Friday nights. And then some Saturday nights. And then long weekends.

Ekon even bought a condo midway between the BBM office and our house, making it easier for their lunch time liaisons, and also for Kaitlin on those long weekends to swing by home for a few hours to be with the kids (and me, I guess).

Kaitlin helped Ekon pick the new condo (it was a hugely expensive place in the trendiest neighborhood), and I could only imagine them smiling and holding hands while touring the area with a real estate agent. Kaitlin began keeping a lot of her clothes at Ekon's place, and my heart dropped whenever I walked into her closet, now half empty.

It also broke my heart to look at the little silver tray on the top of her dresser in our bedroom. Kaitlin always put her wedding and engagement rings on that tray when she was at work or on dates. Nowadays, it seemed like she spent more time ringless than with the rings on her finger.

Kaitlin never denied me sex. In fact, we were having more sex now than ever before. I think it helped her deal with the guilt.

I never complained about their growing relationship, and always put on a brave face, because if I forced her to break up with Ekon we'd just be in that bad place again. And I think I mostly fooled her into thinking I was truly okay with it, like in the past when she was dating and sleeping with Darrin and the other Populars.

But at some level she knew it was different for me now since it was more than just physical. Now there was no denying she was emotionally involved with another man. So, she tried to make it up to me with sex, and despite everything, I loved having sex with her.

Kaitlin had the greatest body. Maybe if I wasn't such a leg man I wouldn't have been so addicted to her, but all it took was hearing the *swish swish* of her nylons as she walked by, or a high heel dangling on her small pretty feet, or even just seeing her sit cross legged with her skirt inching up slightly higher, and my body would fill with lust.

Kaitlin continued to tell me stories of what they did together. She told me because she knew it aroused me, and because I put on a brave face. She didn't realize how much the stories hurt me.

But they did arouse me too, and whenever she started with the stories my lust would turn dark and demented, and I'd get hard, and I'd cum when her stories hurt the most, and because I *did* get so excited and I *did* came when I did, she'd tell me more, thinking I wanted to hear more, saying to me things like, "*God, Ekon's body is so amazing!*" or "*I love the way his big cock stretches me!*" or "*Ekon's got an amazing tongue to, I almost pass out when he goes down on me!*"

And even saying, "*Now I understand when they say once you go black you never go back! I get it now!*"

She wasn't being cruel. She told me because she knew I loved hearing it. And I suspected she didn't mean everything she said, at least not completely; sometimes she said things because it made me moan or my dick get harder, so she was trying to make me happy. She was right. I did love when she said those things.

But it was my dark side that loved it, and after my lust was sated, I'd feel sick inside with a broken heart. Then later, maybe an hour or two later, I'd think about what she said to me, and I'd get hard again, and sometimes I'd drag her into our bed again. Other times I 'd go into the bathroom, sit on the toilet with the seat down, and jerk off thinking of Ekon with his big black cock buried in my wife, and my wife saying things like "Oh god Ekon, you're the best lover I've ever had, I never knew sex could be this good!"

And I came hardest when I imagined Kaitlin saying, "I love you Ekon!"

I knew I was pathetic, but I couldn't help myself. I began to understand what people mean when they say it's hard being married to a beautiful woman. Men pursue those women, even after they're married. And if you're like me, and you have a desire to see your wife with another man, then eventually she's going to fall in love with a man who's more handsome, has a better body, is a better lover, and has more money.

And the fact Kaitlin found all this with a black man ... that she *loved* a black man ... it wasn't something I could compete with. It was bad enough his cock was bigger, he was a better lover, he made more money ... if Kaitlin was into the taboo of being with a black man ... how could I compete with that? Like her, I was lily white.

⸺⬤⸺

KAITLIN CONTINUED TO do well at her job, reaching the highest performance level. As a perk, everyone who reached that level got an all-expense paid trip to Aruba. Kaitlin talked me into going with her. She knew we needed some time together, and even though a lot of the Populars would be there (they still knew me as her cousin), and she had to go on a few BBM team-building outings, she thought we'd be able to spend most of the time together, away from everyone else.

The first three days were great. Kaitlin managed to get an isolated bungalow off the beaten path, so we were alone together, eating room service, sunning and swimming in our bungalow's private pool, but mostly making love and holding each other. It was really good. I had her all to myself, and I felt better than I had in a long time.

Then on the fourth morning, Rachel showed up at our door, out of breath and looking worried. Eyeing me warily, she pulled Kaitlin outside to talk. A few minutes later Kaitlin came back in, and I couldn't read her face.

"Ekon just got here," she told me.

I felt shocked. "You told me he wasn't going to be here!" I snapped.

"He wasn't, he's a partner, this getaway is for non-partners only," she said hurriedly, sensing my rising anger. "I don't know why he's here."

"I've got a good idea why he's here," I said angrily. "So, what are you going to do now?" It came out like a challenge. I knew what her answer would be, what her choice would be, so I just wanted her to tell me. I wanted her to say it to my face.

"Well, I mean, first I'm going to see what he's doing here. But if he's staying—."

"You're going to stay with him!" I finished her sentence angrily, turning away from her.

She grabbed my hand. "No, Connor, I didn't say that!" she said pleadingly. "But we still need this job, and remember people still think you're my cousin. It'd look weird if I didn't see him at all."

"Yeah, you're right," I said with sarcastic bitterness. "They'd think it was strange if you didn't spend all your time with your boyfriend. I'm just your cousin, and he's the man you love."

"Connor, please, let's not get into this now," she begged. "We've had such a good time, it's been good for us. I promise I'll still be with you most of the time. I'll be with Ekon just enough for appearances, I promise."

We stared at each other for long moments, and then I finally gave her a reluctant, terse nod. She gave me an encouraging smile.

"Let me go see what he's doing here, and I'll be right back," she said. She kissed me, squeezed my hand, and then left.

I suspected she wouldn't return soon, and she didn't. A couple of hours later, Rachel stopped by again to pick up Kaitlin's bathing suit.

"She said it was a pink bikini – oh, here it is," Rachel said as she rummaged through Kaitlin's luggage.

"Why'd she send you? Is she too busy fucking Ekon to get it herself?"

Rachel must not have heard the anger and bitterness in my voice, because she laughed. "I guess so. Ekon wasn't supposed to be here, but I guess a week away from your pretty wife's sexy ass was too much for him." Then she looked at me and saw the hurt in my face. "Connor, are you okay?" she asked concerned. "You're not okay, are you?" she said as I turned away.

"I thought you liked this -—lifestyle," Rachel said to my back. "I mean, it surprised me at first because you've always been so uptight – no offense – but I thought you liked it. In fact, I thought you were really into it."

"Maybe I did like it, until she fell in love with him," I said angrily.

Rachel was about to say something when I held out my hand to stop her. I didn't want her pity. I didn't want to hear her say, "Yes, she loves Ekon, but she still loves you too." After all, Ekon was Desirable #1. Rachel was probably happy her BFF was finally with someone she deserved, with someone worthy of a fellow Popular.

"Please, just leave," I snapped.

"Well, okay then, I guess I'll bring this to Kaitlin," she said hesitantly holding the bikini. I gave her a "whatever" shrug and opened the mini-bar to start drinking.

The next morning, I was awakened by a soft hand on my cheek. "Hi sleepyhead," Kaitlin said. She kissed my lips. "I'm sorry I didn't get back yesterday. It got complicated."

"Yeah, I guess love is like that," I said sarcastically, noticing she wore the pink bikini.

"We need to talk, but not now," she said, and then quickly put a finger on my lips to stop me from replying.

She pulled the covers off me and took my cock into her mouth. I'd already been half hard, and I got rigid as soon as I felt her soft tongue on my shaft. She sucked me for a few moments, kneeling on the bed between my legs. She stopped, took off her bottoms - it was no more effort than pulling the strings at each hip - and then straddled me, using her hand to guide me inside her. She felt loose and wet, making it clear Ekon had just fucked her, and she'd obviously let him cum inside her. Did she always let him cum inside her now? It surprised me she wasn't pregnant yet.

"Go ahead, tell me what you did with him!" I hissed, my lust growing despite my hurt and bitterness. "Tell me how much you love fucking him! How much you love his big cock stretching your pussy! Go ahead and tell me!"

"Not now, Connor," Kaitlin said softly, shaking her head, her long silky brown hair with the reddish highlights swaying from side to side. "Let's just be us now."

"Why?" I said angrily, tearing off her bikini top. "Are you going to deny those are Ekon's bite marks on your tits? Are you going to deny those are his hickeys on your neck?"

I rolled Kaitlin over onto her back and pounded her hard. Despite everything, despite my self-loathing, talking about them together got me excited, and I slammed into her again and again, getting close to my orgasm. "Tell me how he loves kissing you! Tell me how he loves your tits, and how he loves your legs! Tell me how he loves you! Tell me! Tell me, damn it, tell me!"

Kaitlin didn't respond to my rants. Moments later I came inside her, adding my sperm to Ekon's. But I was neutered, whereas he was still virile and fertile. And black.

"So now you're going back to him?" I hissed bitterly after we untangled our bodies.

"Connor, I'm not going back to *him*," she said. "But remember, today there's a BBM morning seminar. I've got to go to it, it's a team building thing, it's mandatory. I'll be back after."

Yeah, right, how convenient. "Okay, whatever," I said dismissively.

Kaitlin hesitated, looking like she didn't know what to say to me.

She got into the shower and dressed. She looked incredible of course, her hair up with a pretty bow, lipstick making her lips look wet, a thin sundress that ended way above her knees, and Jimmy Choo high heels with two thin straps (one over her pedicured toes and another around her slim ankles) that really showed off her small pretty feet.

She saw the scowl on my face and answered my unspoken suspicion. "Connor, I'm not wearing this for Ekon. This is how I dress at work. You've seen me dress like this for work a thousand times."

Kaitlin was telling the truth of course. I used to like watching her dress for work. But not anymore. For some time now, it was Ekon who enjoyed her body in her sexy work clothes. Not me. All I got nowadays was the leftovers, the sloppy seconds.

Then I knew she was lying about not dressing for Ekon when I watched as she stuffed a bikini in a bag. She saw my look and sighed in frustration. "BBM has a pool lunch after the seminar. It's mandatory too. I'll be back right after that, I promise."

I turned back to the TV, pretending to watch ESPN.

"I *promise*," Kaitlin repeated kissing my cheek, but I didn't bother to respond, having been on the receiving end of too many broken promises from her. I heard her sigh again, and then I heard the click click of her high heels as she walked across the room and left.

I knew she wouldn't be back, but for some reason I wanted to see for myself. So, at lunch I walked over to the main resort complex. From one of the restaurants, I was able to look at the pool without being seen.

All the Populars were there, and I quickly spotted Kaitlin. She was easy to spot. Despite everything, I couldn't help noticing how incredible she looked.

She'd changed out of the sundress and put on a white bikini that really set off the tan she'd gotten the last few days. It wasn't a dark tan. Kaitlin was too fair and lily white for that. But the bright white bikini really showed off her light tan well.

The white bikini was tiny. The material could have fit in a child's hand. It covered everything, but just barely, giving the impression that at any moment some private part of her would be revealed, which of course meant she attracted the attention of every male eye (and more than a few envious female eyes). I remembered how she had gotten it special for this trip, for me, and thought bitterly how she was now wearing it for Ekon.

Of course, Kaitlin and Ekon were together, like the happy couple they were. She lay on a lounge chaise lounge on her stomach, and Ekon sat next to her. He said something to her. She replied and he laughed, making the people around them laugh.

Then Ekon picked up the suntan lotion and squirted some on her back. He rubbed it in, at one point stopping to untie the back strap of her bikini top.

Kaitlin said something to him, and Ekon laughed again and gave her a slap on her butt. As a partner of BBM, he was breaking office norms and probably some laws by treating an employee that way. He was being incredibly familiar and even intimate with Kaitlin in front of everyone. Although by now, everyone knew they were dating. Ekon was popular – he was Desirable #1 – and Kaitlin wasn't complaining. So, the men were cool with how he was treating Kaitlin, and the women if anything were envious.

Then Ekon rubbed lotion down her long shapely legs. Then he rubbed up her legs to her butt. The bottoms of her bikini wasn't a thong, but still it exposed some of her shapely cheeks. Ekon rubbed lotion over that exposed skin. Even though I was angry and dying inside, it was still incredibly erotic for me to see Ekon's jet black hand rubbing her bare, tanned skin right next to the bright white of her bikini bottoms.

Kaitlin playfully pushed his hands away and impishly nudged him in the ribs. The crowd laughed. Ekon leaned over and whispered something into Kaitlin's ear. She rolled her eyes and shook her head no.

Ekon whispered something to her again. As he did, he rubbed more lotion on her back with his fingers. This time his fingertips slipped down her side and lightly swept across the swell of her perfect breasts (the sides of her breasts were exposed since her bikini top was untied).

Kaitlin looked sideways at Ekon as he caressed her this way. As she looked at her black lover, I saw clearly into her face. She looked aroused. Ekon's caresses and flirting were getting to her.

Ekon whispered into her ear again. She whispered something back. He nodded, like he agreed to whatever she just said.

After a long moment – like Kaitlin was considering whatever Ekon had whispered to her – she stood up and began walking away, taking care to first re-tie her top and adjust her bottoms. Ekon gave a last grin to the crowd of Populars at the pool. Then he stood up and followed Kaitlin.

All the Populars grinned and gossiped as Kaitlin and Ekon walked away. They knew what was about to happen. So did I.

Kaitlin stopped to whisper something to Rachel. Rachel nodded. Then Kaitlin continued walking with Ekon following close behind.

I knew Kaitlin wasn't returning to me after the pool lunch. She was going to Ekon's room to let him fuck her.

It was another broken promise. I was angry. My heart was broken. I felt betrayed. And manipulated.

I felt like my marriage was over. This was too much. A man can only take so much. This was the end.

I went back to my room and packed. There was no reason to stay.

Even though I was furious at Kaitlin, by heart was breaking. I was destroyed. There were tears in my eyes as I packed. Honestly, I thought about suicide. But no. I would never do that to my children.

Then I thought – maybe what happened at the pool was all a misunderstanding. Kaitlin and I had been married for years. We've been together longer counting dating and the year we were engaged before our wedding. We loved each other. We were soul mates.

She *didn't* lie to me. She *wasn't* with Ekon right now. It was something else. There had to be an explanation. An innocent explanation. The kind of thing we'd laugh about later.

I found out where Ekon was staying. Like us, it was a bungalow on the outskirts of the resort. That information was private of course, but I gave a cabana boy $100 and had the information within minutes.

I made my way over to Ekon's bungalow. I expected it to be empty. *Kaitlin's not with him,* I told myself.

Or maybe she was, but it was work. Maybe other partners were here, maybe even her boss Morgan was here. Maybe that's why Ekon showed up unexpectedly. Maybe there was a big deal BBM was working on, and they were pulling key people together. That would certainly include Kaitlin, especially if Morgan was here.

It has to be this, I told myself. That would explain everything. Kaitlin loved me. I was the father of her children. She would never hurt me that way.

Ekon's bungalow was similar to ours. In the back, it was all glass with a pool and patio. Dense foliage bordered the patio. Looking through the dense trees and plants, I could see clearly into Ekon's bungalow, pool and patio without risk of being seen.

My heart sank as soon as I looked through the trees. Kaitlin *was* with Ekon. And they were alone. They were having sex.

They were outside on a big circular lounge next to the private pool. I wasn't more than 20 feet away from them. So, I could see everything. Hear everything.

Both Kaitlin and Ekon were completely naked. Except she had her high heels on, the ones she put on that morning with the sundress. She'd been wearing flip flops when she left the pool, with Ekon following close behind. So, Kaitlin had switched from flip flops to high heels.

For Ekon.

So, he could fuck her in heels.

Ekon was on his back on the lounger. Kaitlin was on top. Moving up and down on his big black cock.

Ekon wasn't wearing a condom. Again, Kaitlin had let this black man put his black dick into her bare. I was sure she would let him cum inside her again. Let him shoot jets of his black sperm into her. Kaitlin was not on any protection. I was shocked she wasn't pregnant yet. Or maybe she was. Maybe she just hadn't told me yet.

"Your pussy feels so good," Ekon moaned as Kaitlin moved up and down his long, thick shaft. He was looking at her face and body while she fucked him. His big black hands cupped her perfect, lily white breasts, fondling them and rubbing her nipples.

"You feel so good baby," Kaitlin moaned. Her face was flushed and her eyes heavy-lidden, reflections of her arousal. "You feel *so good* inside me. You shouldn't be here. But I'm glad you're here. I missed your cock. I missed *you.*"

"I know you told me to give you and Connor space," Ekon said as they continued to slowly fuck.

No. Fuck wasn't the right word.

As they slowly made love.

"But I needed to see you," Ekon said. "I missed you."

"I missed you too baby," Kaitlin cooed. "Being alone with Connor was good. But I was thinking about you all the time. I even thought about you when we made love."

"Oh god, that's so hot babe," Ekon moaned.

"No, it's not," Kaitlin said looking regretful. "I feel terrible."

"Don't feel bad, Kaitlin," Ekon said. "If we met first, you'd be with me, not him."

"Don't say things like that," Kaitlin said looking sad.

"It's true and you know it," Ekon said. "Have you told Connor? What we talked about?"

"I can't do that to him."

"But I love you," Ekon said. "And you love me too, right?"

"Yes, I love you so much," Kaitlin said without any hesitation. "But the kids. Connor is a good husband, and a good father."

"I know he's a good man—."

"He *is* a good man," Kaitlin said.

"Let me meet your kids," Ekon said. From his tone of voice, it wasn't the first time they talked about this. "They'll like me."

"I can't do that to Connor," Kaitlin said.

"I'll be like an uncle," Ekon said. "I won't try to replace Connor. I promise."

"I don't know ...," Kaitlin said, looking uncertain.

"So, you'll talk to him?" Ekon asked after a few moments.

Kaitlin paused, then said, "I'll ... I'll try."

"But Ekon," she said urgently. "We have to finish. I need to get back to Connor. He's waiting for me."

"Okay. I'm almost there."

"I am too."

"I love you Kaitlin," Ekon said.

"I love you too, Ekon," Kaitlin said. Then they hugged and kissed as they continued to make love.

I couldn't watch or hear anymore. I staggered away.

Somehow, I made it back to my bungalow. I was destroyed. Heartbroken. Dead inside.

I was only mildly surprised to see Rachel at the door of my bungalow. She jumped up as I approached.

"Hey Connor, where have you been?" Rachel asked.

"Around," I managed to say.

"Oh. Okay," Rachel said. She saw my tortured face and looked uncertain. "Anyways, Kaitlin asked me to let you know she has a Zoom call with old man Morgan. She'll be here right after. You know how he is. He works her 24/7. But at least the pay is good, right?"

"Yeah, right," I said dismissively. I pushed past Rachel and went into my bungalow, locking the door behind me.

So, not only did Kaitlin break her promise to me. Not only did she betray me. Not only did she destroy me.

She sent her friend to lie on her behalf.

That was it. That's the end. A man can only take so much. If there was any hope for our marriage, it was gone.

Our marriage was over.

———◆———

I GRABBED MY SUITCASE and took a taxi to the airport. On the way though, I found out the next flight home wasn't until the morning, so I was stuck here for the evening.

I told the driver to take me into town. I walked around, killing time.

Then I went to a bar. It had a view of the ocean, and I stared into it, feeling numb. The sun went down, and the view was so incredible it brought me out of my stupor, if only for a few moments.

You know how it is, when something like that amazing sunset strikes you like that, and you forget where you are, and what's going on in your life? Well, at that moment, I thought how great it would be if Kaitlin was there next to me, because we always liked watching sunsets together, holding hands, sipping wine, just being next to each other, not talking, just comfortable and feeling good in each other's company. Then I snapped out of it, remembered where I was, where Kaitlin was and who she was with, what she'd done to me, what she'd done to us, and realized there wouldn't be any more sunsets for us.

The bartender came by, and I guess he saw the tear running down my cheek, and he offered to buy me a free one. He poured it, and I drank, and then I told him the story, everything, from Kaitlin getting the job at BBM and me pretending to be her cousin, all the way to right now, me sitting here in his bar.

He was a nice man, and he let me get it all out, and he patted my shoulder when the tears came, and finally he let me crash for a few hours on the couch in his office. The next morning when I woke up, this kind bartender was there with a cup of coffee, and he drove me to the airport and wished me good luck.

I don't know ... you meet people sometimes, they're in and out of your life, but he was a friend when I really needed a friend. He didn't have any advice for me, or wisdom to solve all my problems. But he was a friend.

I got to the airport and checked in, and then walked over to the gate. I sat down and closed my eyes, still numb, not wanting to think about what I'd lost, what I was going to do next. I didn't know what I was going to do next.

All I knew was my marriage was over. Me and Kaitlin, we were over.

"You were going to leave without me?" I hear a quivering voice say, and I opened my eyes.

It was Kaitlin. She was dressed in the sundress from yesterday. "I got back to the room after lunch, just like I promised. But you were gone, and your suitcase was gone. I've been waiting for you here all night."

"Kaitlin, no more lies, okay?" I said. I was exhausted and emotionally spent. "I saw everything. I saw you at the pool. And saw you with Ekon at his room. I heard everything too. So, no more lies. Okay? At least give me that."

Kaitlin sat next to be and began sobbing. "I'm sorry, I'm sorry ...," she said over and over again between tears.

That's what she always did when we had an argument. She'd cry and then I'd take her into my arms. We'd make love, and the argument would be over. But not this time.

Not this time.

"It's over Kaitlin," I told her. "You love Ekon. Maybe you still love me. I'll give you that. But he's your man now. Not me. And it's been that way for a long time. Let's both face reality and move on with our lives."

"What are you saying?" Kaitlin said through teary eyes. She looked shocked and horrified. And scared.

"What do you mean, what am I'm saying?" I said back. "We'll get a divorce. Then you can marry Ekon. Or whatever. I don't care anymore."

"But I don't want that!" Kaitlin cried, sobbing again and grabbing for me. I pulled away and stood up. My flight was boarding.

"I'll get the kids from your parents," I told her. "Stay here as long as you want. Don't worry. I won't steal them or try to get sole custody. We'll work out something fair. My lawyer will contact you."

"No, Connor, no!" Kaitlin cried. She ran after me. The flight crew held her back since she didn't have a ticket.

I boarded my plane without looking back.

⎯⎯⎯⎯●⎯⎯⎯⎯

EPILOGUE – 7 MONTHS LATER

We met at a coffee place. I had ignored all her calls and texts. It was the first time we'd seen each other or even spoken since the airport.

Rachel had been the go-between. She shuffled the kids between us so I wouldn't have to see or talk to Kaitlin. I figured Rachel owed me that much. She was complicit in all this and lied to my face. To her credit, she agreed to be our go-between even though it took a lot of work running the kids between me and Kaitlin.

Kaitlin, though, told my lawyer through her lawyer that she would not cooperate with the divorce and settlement without talking to me. My lawyer knew I hated Kaitlin. He said, "Talk to her Connor. What does it matter? Then we can finish the divorce and you can get on with your life."

So, I met Kaitlin for coffee.

She looked beautiful and sexy as always, although sad, anxious and scared. I was surprised to see she wasn't pregnant. Or wearing Ekon's engagement ring. Whatever. I didn't care anymore.

As soon as we sat, Kaitlin apologized over and over again. She said she knew she had fucked up, gone too far, lied to me, betrayed me, treated me like shit, ruined our marriage. She said she still loved me. She still wanted me. She missed me terribly and cried almost every day. She asked if there was anything she could do to get me to reconsider divorcing her. To get me to take her back.

"Are you still with Ekon?" I asked her.

"I'm not *with* him," Kaitlin said. Then with downcast eyes, she admitted, "I still see him."

"Then why would I ever take you back?" I snapped with a glare at her.

Kaitlin winced at my harsh tone and glare like it was a physical blow. She said desperately, "Please let me finish. Please let me say everything I want to say. Then if you still want to divorce, I'll sign the papers. Okay?"

Still glaring at her, I nodded tersely.

"I can't resist Ekon," Kaitlin said through teary eyes. "I've tried. It's not like with Darren. Or anyone I've ever been with before. I think it's because ... I think it's because he's black. There's something about black men. You know what they say. It's true, I think. It's not just Ekon either. It's all black men. I notice them now. I never did before. It was like, before, they were in the background. But now I look at black men more than white men. It's like how you're attracted to girls with nice legs. I'm attracted to black men."

"Why are you telling me this?" I asked with exasperation. I didn't understand. Why did Kaitlin think telling me this would want me to take her back? Did she forget *I* was white?

"I don't want to *be* with a black man!" Kaitlin said pleadingly through teary eyes. "I don't love a black man! I love you!"

"That's a lie!" I hissed. "You love Ekon! I heard you!"

"What I feel for Ekon is complicated," Kaitlin said, trying to explain her feelings to me. "I don't know *what* I feel for him. I just know I can't resist him. Physically. But I can't live without you in my life, Connor. I love you. Real love, not just sex. Real love. Don't you still love me? Even a little? Are you happy without me?"

I looked away. No, I wasn't happy. I was miserable. I was dead inside.

"What did Ekon want you to talk to me about?" I asked her. "When you were fucking by his pool. He wanted you to talk to me about something."

"Ekon likes how things were," Kaitlin told me. "He likes dating married white girls. He dates single girls too, but only white girls. He's into that."

"Into what?"

Kaitlin shrugged. "He calls it blacking white girls."

I stared at the coffee in my hand, processing all this.

"Anyways, he wanted you to get more involved when we were together," Kaitlin said. "That's what he wanted me to talk to you about. He wanted you to come on our dates. Stay at his apartment when I was there."

"Why?"

"I told him how you watched from the closet that first time, and he got so excited," Kaitlin said. "He said white girls who are married are the best. He says he likes to show white husbands how much better he is. In bed. It's an ego thing, I guess."

I stared at Kaitlin. I was having a hard time grasping all of this.

"It sounded like you didn't want to talk to me about it," I finally said.

"I didn't want him to humiliate you, Connor," Kaitlin said pleadingly. "I think that's what he wants to do. He gets off on that. And in the heat of the moment, I don't trust myself. I might not defend you. I might even go along with it. I didn't want to do that."

I stared at Kaitlin, trying to look inside her. Was it true? Had she really been on my side the whole time?

"Why did Ekon want to meet our kids?" I asked.

"He wants to meet our kids, our friends, our parents," Kaitlin said. "He wants to go on vacations with us. He wants to get into our lives. That turns him on too. He wants people we know suspecting I might be having an affair with him. He wants to fuck me while we're at a neighborhood party. He likes those mind games. It's more than just physical sex with him. He calls it "mindfucks."

I thought about our friends, our families, everyone we knew, seeing Ekon around and thinking he was having an affair with Kaitlin. I thought about how they would think I couldn't satisfy my wife, so she turned to another man – a black man – for sexual pleasure.

I slowly sipped my coffee as these thoughts ran through my head.

"So, how would it work if we got back together?" I asked after a few long moments.

"It would be like before," Kaitlin said, looking hopeful that I seemed to be considering taking her back. "I know I went too far before. So, it would be just Friday or Saturday, not both. Except I would still sleep over that night, and see him at work, and sometimes Ekon would take me away for a long weekend, but only after you gave permission. And you're welcome to be there for all of it. On our dates, at his apartment, on the long weekends. Since the kids are starting school soon, you can even be there at his apartment if we do something in the afternoon. Ekon said he'd even give you a key to his apartment. I'd always let you know what I'm doing. And he promises to respect our space. I told him showing up at the BBM getaway was wrong, and he gets it."

"But you missed him, right?" I said bitterly, remembering what she'd said while fucking Ekon at his bungalow. "You were thinking about him. Even when we were making love."

Kaitlin winced like I'd hit her. "Does it help that I think about you when I'm with him? Connor, you're all I've thought about since you left me at that airport."

"Right. Except when Ekon's fucking you," I snapped bitterly.

"Connor ... I'm trying to explain to you," Kaitlin said, her eyes tearing up. "I can't help it. I can't resist him. But I don't love him. I love *you*. I want to be with *you*. I want to be married to *you*."

We stared at each other for long moments.

Finally, I said, "So, if we get back together, are you with him for the rest of our lives?

"I'm not with *him*," Kaitlin said, correcting me again. "If you take me back, I'll be with *you*. I don't know how long Ekon will be around. Maybe I'll get over my ... fetish, for black men. I don't know ... all this is new to me."

"I'm frankly surprised you're not pregnant yet," I said as I crossed my arms defiantly.

"I almost always make Ekon wear a condom. And when he doesn't, I make him pull out," Kaitlin said. "You may not believe me, but it's the truth. And no, I'm not lying and got an abortion, if that's what you're wondering. You know I could never do that."

"So, if Ekon got you pregnant, you'd have a half black baby?"

"Connor, I *told you* I make him use condoms," Kaitlin implored. "And I've taken morning-after pills. You know that."

"Answer my question," I insisted.

"You know what I believe," Kaitlin said. "So yes, I would have the baby. It would be *your* baby. But if you wanted, I'd give it up for adoption. It would break my heart though."

I looked away, both shamed and angry by what she said. I snapped, "Maybe *I* should get the vasectomy reversed and fuck *my* baby into you."

Kaitlin said, "If you take me back and I'm your wife again, you can do anything you want to me. I'm your wife. My body belongs to you, Connor. *You. Only you.*"

"So, if I want you to let Rachel fuck you with a strap-on, you'll do it?" I joked.

"Yes, I'd do it," Kaitlin agreed immediately, looking serious. "I'll do anything to get you back. *Anything.* You can't touch Rachel though. Or do anything but watch. I couldn't handle that. I don't want an open marriage. I can't stand the thought of you with another girl."

"So, it's one way with you, is that it?" I said bitterly.

"If that's what it takes to get you back, then okay, you can be with other girls," Kaitlin said softly, looking tearful. "But I won't like it. I won't be happy. It doesn't get me hot like it gets you hot."

I shrugged. I didn't want another girl. I never had. I only wanted Kaitlin.

"Have you ... been with other girls?" she hesitantly asked.

I didn't answer. No, I had not. But I wasn't going to tell her that. I wasn't going to give her the satisfaction.

Kaitlin looked sad when I didn't answer. With a tear down her cheek, she said, "I guess I don't want to know."

I stared at her for long moments. Then I made my decision.

I said, "Okay. We'll give it a try."

Kaitlin's face brightened, like a beautiful sunrise coming up over a field of glorious flowers. "Really?" she said with a big, schoolgirlish, giddy smile.

I smiled back. It was my first real smile in over 7 months. "Yes. Really," I said.

"Come on," I said, grabbing her hand. I took her to my apartment where I'd lived for the last 7 months. It wasn't too far away.

Ekon had had Kaitlin all to himself for 7 months. I wanted to reclaim her.

As my wife.

And I grinned as I thought about a girl-girl scene between my wife and Rachel. It had always been a fantasy of mine to see the beautiful BFFs together.

This could be fun.

Yes, I still had to deal with Ekon. But maybe I could handle it better if Kaitlin and I communicated better.

And to be honest, some of the things Ekon wanted to do ... well, they titillated me. I wasn't sure if I wanted to go down that path, or how far. I realized it might be a slippery slope that once you went down, it might be hard to come back.

But I would at least give it some thought.

For now, I wanted sex with my wife. And I had a machoistic curiosity to find out how loose her pussy was after fucking Ekon's big black cock exclusively for 7 months.

At the end, would we have a happy ending?

I didn't know. But at least I had Kaitlin back. For now, at least.

DESIRING ANOTHER MAN'S WIFE

I felt nervous, this being our first function at the club. My wife Maddie and I didn't fit into this crowd of ultra-rich people. We joined this exclusive country club about a month ago so I could get to know people like this, to help me at work.

Maddie looked as nervous as me. Not only were we poor compared to all these rich people, but also much younger. I was 29 and Maddie 26, while everyone else was at least 15 years older.

I chatted with a distinguished black man who introduced himself as Victor. As we spoke, my attention was drawn to a beautiful woman standing across the room. She was tall with long dark hair and wore an elegant off-the-shoulder cocktail dress that ended about mid-thigh.

Unlike my blonde wife Maddie, who's petite and small breasted, this woman had a classic hourglass figure, with large breasts and curvy hips. Her legs weren't slim like Maddie's, but they were shapely and looked great in her stiletto high heels.

The woman eased herself into a seat at the bar. She ordered a drink, and as she did she crossed her legs. This made her dress hike up her thighs, but she quickly adjusted and pulled her dress back down her legs.

My eyes grew wide. For an instant, just before the woman pulled her dress down, her stocking tops were exposed, the dark welts of the sheer nude nylons straining against the straps of her black garter belt.

I've never known a woman who wore real stockings, the kind that's held up with a garter belt. I've seen them often enough in adult movies or on the internet, but I've never met a woman who wore them in public, in real life. I've encouraged Maddie to wear them, but in our entire relationship she's worn them only once, on our wedding day. Usually she goes without hose, or wears pantyhose, like tonight.

I felt myself stiffening, my full attention drawn to the woman. She looked to be Latino, with a dark exotic complexion. Her lips were full and painted bright red, and her large breasts almost spilled over the top of her strapless dress. My eyes focused on her legs. I hoped she'd cross her legs again, so I could glimpse her stocking tops again.

Victor saw my distraction and followed my eyes to the sensual woman. He smiled knowingly and gestured to the woman. The woman looked at Victor, and then at me. She smiled. She slipped off the chair, and once again I glimpsed a hint of her stocking tops. Then she began walking towards us. The ballroom was loud, but I imagined hearing the click-click of her high heels as she elegantly walked across the hardwood floor towards us.

I panicked. Victor had caught me ogling this sensuous woman, and now he was going to embarrass me in front of everyone. I looked around for Maddie, and found her just a few feet away, speaking to another couple. I hoped her conversation would continue while I dealt with this situation.

The woman arrived and stood in front of us, an almost teasing smile on her full painted lips. In her high heels she was taller than me but came to just Victor's chest.

"Sofia," Victor said, gesturing to me. "I'd like you to meet Adam."

Then Victor looked at me. "Adam, this is Sofia, my wife."

His wife?! My cheeks flushed red in embarrassment. "Hi, ah, nice to meet you," I managed to say as I extended my hand.

Sofia took my hand in hers, her touch light. "The pleasure is mine," she said as she looked into my eyes. Then, just before releasing my hand, she dug her long red nails into my palm. Sparks ran up my spine, and I gratefully grabbed a glass of wine from a passing waiter.

Sofia looked questioning behind me. "Where's your lovely wife? Madison, isn't it?"

"That's right," I said, surprised. How did she know my wife's name? But then I remembered the club emailed a newsletter listing all the new members, with our pictures. I turned and gestured to Maddie. "Honey, this is Victor and Sofia."

Maddie shook their hands, and we chatted about ourselves, while they entertained us with gossip about the club and its members. Victor and Sofia made a physically striking couple. He looked like he stepped out of *GQ*, and she *Vogue* magazine.

The cover band played a popular song, and Sofia took my hand. "Maddie, you don't mind if I dance with your husband, do you?"

Maddie looked a little tipsy, having had more than her share of wine. "Not at all," she said with a friendly lopsided smile.

"No need to worry," Victor said to me as he waved us away. "I'll keep your wife company."

I led Sofia onto the crowded dance floor. Feeling awkward, I took Sofia's hand in mine. Then, I hesitantly placed my other hand on her hip, making sure to stay well above the swell of her shapely ass.

Sofia smiled and we began to dance. She was an excellent dancer, sensually swaying to the music. The silky, barely-there material of her dress left little to the imagination, and I quickly realized she wasn't wearing a bra. I also felt the outline of her garter belt around her waist, and the effect on me (and my manhood) was what you'd expect.

The growing crowd pressed us together. I was embarrassed; certain Sofia could feel my erection pressing against her stomach. But she didn't pull away. If anything, Sofia pressed closer against me. I looked down, seeing the swells of her large breasts. Her hard, braless nipples caused dents in the filmy material of her dress. Sofia saw me looking down her dress. She looked into my eyes and smiled invitingly.

The dance ended, and I let Sofia go. Not because I wanted to, but because I didn't know what else to do. "We ... ah ... I guess we better get back."

Sofia smiled seductively. She reached inside my jacket and ran her long red nails along my side. "Wouldn't you like to take me for a walk? The moon is lovely tonight."

My body tingled from Sofia's touch. And my head spun. Was she propositioning me? "Um ... I ... ah ... I better get back to Maddie."

Sofia pouted. "Alright," she finally said, sounding disappointed, but not angry. Then she took my arm and let me lead her back to our spouses.

Later that night, I fucked my wife like I hadn't fucked her in years. As soon as we got home, I threw Maddie onto the sofa, pushing her dress up around her waist while simultaneously pulling my cock out of my pants. I pulled her pantyhose and panties down her legs, not bothering to take them off completely, and then rammed my rock-hard cock into her pussy. It didn't take me long to cum. I would've felt guilty except Maddie came just as fast, which surprised me.

We went to our bedroom and made love again. Again, this surprised me. To be honest, our sex life hadn't been good for a while. We've been together for 8 years, married for 5, and like most married couples our sex life waned after a few years. Nowadays we might do it once a week, but often only as the culmination of watching a porn movie on the TV. So, doing it twice in less than an hour really surprised me.

I knew what got me so hot. It was Sofia. But Maddie's sudden passion surprised me. It didn't take long before I understood why.

After our lovemaking, we spooned in bed. Maddie was so quiet I assumed she had fallen asleep.

"I need to tell you something," she finally said, trepidation in her voice.

"What?"

Maddie turned to face me, looking nervous. "Tonight ... while you were dancing with Sofia. Victor made a pass at me."

I almost jumped off the bed. "What?! What did he do?"

Maddie hesitated, then finally said, "After you left with Sofia, he asked me to dance. I must've been a little drunk, because I didn't notice as he led me into a side room." Maddie described how Victor had kissed and fondled her. He groped her tits and reached under her dress.

"How far did he go?" I asked angrily, picturing Victor's black hand between my wife's legs.

"He ... he cupped me," Maddie said.

"But then I pushed him away," she quickly added. "And I ran out of the room."

Anger flared inside me. How dare Victor take advantage of my wife!

But then something Maddie said struck me. "What do you mean, *then* you pushed him away?" I said accusingly. "You weren't fighting before that? You let him touch you?"

"Adam, no," Maddie pleaded, gripping my arm. "It wasn't like that at all. I guess I was drunk. It took me a minute to realize what was happening. As soon as I did, I pushed him away and ran from the room."

I let it go, not challenging Maddie further. But I wondered if she was holding back and not telling me the full truth. Victor had aroused her. That's why she had been so horny tonight. I felt jealous, and mad. I considered telling Maddie about Sofia, but something held me back. I spooned Maddie again, and with the assurance of my arm around her, she quickly fell asleep. But I laid awake late into the night, thinking of Sofia.

⸻ ● ⸻

I COULDN'T GET MY MIND off Sofia. I masturbated more than once fantasizing about her, and the next time Maddie and I made love, I orgasmed thinking of Sofia.

I was still mad at Victor for groping Maddie, but it also mystified me why he'd risk a pass at another woman when he had a wife like Sofia.

Don't get me wrong. My wife is pretty, and she keeps in shape. Her breasts are shapely (although small), her stomach is flat, and she has great legs.

But Sofia is something else. While Maddie is pretty in a cute kind of way, Sofia's beauty is sensual and sophisticated. While Maddie is slim and petite, Sofia is curvy and voluptuous.

My wife dresses conservatively. She usually wears pants, and when she wears a skirt, it goes to her knees. She never wears tight jeans or snug sweaters. Her lingerie is full coverage, cotton bras and panties. She never dresses to take advantage of her best features—her tight ass and long legs. I've encouraged her to dress nicer, but she never has. The funny thing is, Maddie's not a prude. I wasn't her first lover. She doesn't mind giving me head, and she likes watching adult movies with me as foreplay to sex. It's just not in my wife's nature to think about dressing sexy.

I couldn't stop thinking about Sofia. I remembered the charge I felt when I realized Sofia was braless under her strapless dress. I don't think Maddie's ever gone braless. And I remembered the feel of Sofia's garter belt as my hand rested on her waist, and the glimpses I got of Sofia's stocking tops. All that aroused me.

The next club mixer was a week away. I felt guilty for thinking so much about Sofia, so I took some money out of the bank and encouraged Maddie to get a new outfit for the event. The night of the mixer, I barely managed to hide my disappointment when Maddie walked out of our bedroom. She had bought another shapeless, knee length black dress. I inwardly sighed, knowing with certainly what she wore underneath. Black cotton bra, black cotton panties, and black pantyhose. But I was encouraged when I saw Maddie's new shoes. Usually, she wears flats or low heeled pumps. But she had bought black patent leather high heels. They must have been 2 or even 3 inches high. Not exactly fuck-me-pumps, but sexier than she'd ever worn before, and they made her shapely legs look even better.

Victor and Sofia greeted us as soon as we walked into the crowded club, and they insisted we sit at their table. Things were a little awkward at first, but after a few drinks the tension seemed to pass.

I had trouble keeping my eyes off Sofia. She wore a tight black satin dress that was held up by two thin spaghetti straps. The dress ended around mid-thigh, and her long legs were encased in sheer black stockings. The dress was so tight I could clearly see the bumps of her garter straps. I was grateful for the floor length tablecloth, to hide the tent in my pants. I feared Maddie would notice all my glances at Sofia, but thankfully her attention seemed drawn elsewhere.

I had just raised my glass to my lips, when I felt a sharp object press against the soft leather of my shoe. I immediately recognized the pressure as the stiletto of a high heel. Was Maddie playing with me under the table? She hadn't done anything like that before. I looked at my wife across the table. She and Victor were talking, her expression serious. It wasn't her.

But that meant it was Sofia. I glanced at her. She looked at me briefly, but then turned away, a smile on her face. It *was* her!

I pictured in my mind her shoes. They were black stilettos, like the ones Maddie had just purchased, but higher, maybe 4 inches, and they showed a lot of toe cleavage. The reality of Sofia pressing those sexy heels against me got me even harder.

As if to read my thoughts, Sofia dug her stiletto hard into my shoe, so hard I almost yelped in pain. The pressure eased, leaving me feeling disappointed. But then I felt the pointy toe of Sofia's heels touch my ankle. Sofia slowly ran that pointy toe up the leg of my pants, moving up past my sock until it pressed against the bare skin of my calf. My cock throbbed in my pants. She touched me like that for a few moments, and then she pulled away. I thought the game had ended, and part of me was glad, as my heart pounded so wildly I feared a heart attack.

But then I felt her touch again. But when I realized what she was doing I almost came in my pants. She had slipped off her shoe, and now her stockinged foot was traveling up my leg. My cock pressed so hard against my pants it hurt. For the next 5 minutes, Sofia caressed me with her foot. Chills ran up my spine as she scrapped the seam of her stockings that ran along her toes over my bare skin.

I feared Maddie would notice my heavy breathing, and the beads of sweat on my forehead. Thankfully she was still distracted by her conversation with Victor.

Abruptly, Maddie pulled her chair back and got up. "I have to go to the ladies room," she said, looking a little flushed.

"I'll go with you," said Sofia cheerfully. Sofia hesitated a moment—I knew she was putting her heels back on under the table—and then she walked with Maddie to the ladies room.

I felt awkward around Victor, having played footsies with his wife just moments ago. He looked at me, and I prepared myself for his accusations.

But then he smiled, and leaned across the table, like he wanted to share a secret. "My wife is very attracted to you," he said.

I blushed red, shocked at his words and embarrassed at being caught. "What? I'm not sure what you're talking about."

"It's okay Adam," he said, still smiling. "No need to worry, I'm cool. Sofia and I have an arrangement."

"What do you mean?" I asked, knowing how stupid I must sound.

"An arrangement. I suppose you'd call it an open marriage."

"An open marriage?" I said, shocked. "You mean, you and Sofia sleep with other people?"

"Well, not *sleep*," Victor said, laughing. "But I think you get the picture."

Victor's tone became serious. "Like I said, Sofia's attracted to you. *Very* attracted to you. I mean, you're all she's talked about since we met you. And I'm fairly certain you're attracted to her. So, if you'd like to get together with her, I'll be okay with that."

I was momentarily speechless, not believing a woman as alluring and sensuous as Sofia could be attracted to me. "Don't you get jealous? Your wife, attracted to another man? Having sex with another man?"

Victor shrugged. "Like I said, we have an open marriage. It works both ways."

My eyes narrowed. "Soooo ... you want to sleep with Maddie?"

He shook his head. "It doesn't have to be that way. I'm attracted to your wife, sure, she's cute. But if she's not into it, or if you'd rather not tell her, then it could be just you and Sofia." He smiled conspiratorially at me. "Adam, to tell you the truth, Sofia's insatiable; she wants sex all the time. You'd be doing me a favor by spending the night with her. I'd turn on ESPN and have a few beers and watch the game."

"I, ah, I don't know. We've never done anything like this. And I've never cheated on Maddie."

Victor shrugged. "You only live once, buddy," he said. "Sofia's a special girl. You know, she used to be a model? She was in a couple of *Sports Illustrated* swimsuit issues, about 10 years ago. What I'm saying is ... look, Maddie's a sweet girl. She's cute, and she probably turns heads now and then. But Sofia's special. When she walks into a room, every male dick gets hard. She's had that effect on you, right? So, you know what I mean. Well my friend, Sofia wants you, but she's a fickle bitch. If you wait too long, she may be on to the next guy. So, think about it, but don't think too long."

I *did* think about it, later that night as I made love to Maddie, the memory of Sofia's stiletto heels against my bare flesh still fresh in my mind. Once again Maddie seemed more passionate than usual, and I wondered if Victor had played with her under the table, the way Sofia had played with me. The thought of Victor's large black hands on my lily white wife bothered me, but my burning lust for Sofia pushed away those jealous feelings.

I've always been a jealous husband. Maddie and I met in college. I was a bookish, geeky junior, and she a leggy blonde, a popular freshman and former high school prom queen and cheerleader. I tutored her in math, and by the end of the year we were a couple. Her friends were shocked she liked me, and to tell you the truth, so was I. I guess it's true opposites attract. Back in college, guys hit on her all the time, and that continued after we married. It always bothered me, but I'm certain she's never cheated on me, and I've never cheated on her. I've never even considered having sex with another woman.

Until now.

My lust for Sofia consumed me. How could I be so vulnerable to Sofia's charms? Maybe because my sex life with Maddie had cooled. They say married couples go through phases, but this phase had lasted over 2 years. We still loved each other, and were even thinking about kids. Maddie had gone off the pill a few months ago. We weren't trying to get pregnant, but we weren't trying not to either. But while the love remained, the passion had left our relationship.

Maybe the lack of passion in my marriage helped fuel my lust for Sofia. I couldn't get her out of my mind. I found those SI swimsuit issues on the internet, and when I saw the pictures of Sofia my jaw dropped. She was magnificent, wearing skimpy string bikinis that left little to the imagination. She hadn't aged much. Maybe her face looked a little older now, but she was still beautiful, and her breasts were still large and firm, her stomach flat, her ass tight and her legs long and shapely.

I was hugely disappointed when Maddie said she didn't want to go to the next club mixer. She didn't offer an explanation. Instead of going to the club, we went to dinner and a movie. The phone rang as soon as we got home.

"Hello Adam," I heard Victor say on the phone. "Sofia and I missed you and Maddie tonight. We're in your neighborhood. We'd love to stop by to say hello."

I put my hand over the phone, my heart racing. "It's Victor," I said to Maddie, trying to hide my excitement. "He and Sofia are in the neighborhood and asked to stop by."

Maddie looked like a deer caught in the headlights, her face a mixture of surprise, apprehension, excitement and fear. But, being so blinded by my lust for Sofia, Maddie's reaction didn't register with me. I was trying so hard to hide my excitement of seeing Victor's wife again, I wasn't paying attention to the signs from my own wife.

"We should invite them over," I said, trying to sound nonchalant. "They're just down the street. We don't want to be rude."

Maddie started to say something, and then shrugged, looking resigned. I smiled excitedly and told Victor to come up to our apartment.

"I guess I better change," Maddie said. I didn't know what she meant. We'd just gotten home from our date night, and Maddie was already dressed for an evening out, in a skirt and blouse, and pumps.

But I nodded and said, "Sure," happy that Maddie had agreed to Victor and Sofia's visit.

Maddie disappeared for about 15 minutes, and when she emerged from our bedroom my jaw almost dropped. She looked fantastic! She wore a snug fitting turtleneck, and a short skirt. A mini-skirt! I couldn't remember the last time Maddie wore anything so short, and the skirt did a great job showing off her long shapely legs. She had put on hose (pantyhose, I was sure), and also the high heels she wore to the last club mixer.

"You look great, honey," I said, still shocked at what I saw. "Is that a new outfit?"

She nodded hesitantly. "Um ... yeah. I had some money left over after buying these shoes. Do you like?"

I began to nod, but then the door buzzed. I opened the door and shook hands with Victor, and then he passed me to greet Maddie. As he did I got my first glimpse of Sofia.

It would not be an exaggeration to say she looked breathtaking. She wore a form fitting red dress that swooped in the front and plunged in the back. She wore black hose and black high heels. Her hair was up, treating me to an unimpeded view of her long, graceful neck. She greeted me with a kiss on the cheek, and I was engulfed in her sensuous perfume.

Sofia's soft full lips lingered on my cheek, making me almost shudder with excitement. Then Sofia trailed her lips lightly across my cheek towards my lips, but at the last moment she teasingly pulled away. I glanced nervously behind Sofia, fearful of my wife's anger. But Victor had taken Maddie with him into the kitchen to make drinks.

Sofia took my arm and led me to the sofa. Her dress was so short it couldn't possibly hide her lace top stockings. I was certain she wore pantyhose underneath because her skirt was so short. But when she sat and crossed her legs, I was treated to a glimpse of her stocking tops.

Sofia took my hand and placed it on her thigh. I felt the outline of her garter straps.

I didn't need to touch her back to know she was braless, as I'd done that first time when we danced. The back of her dress plunged to just above her ass. There was no way she could be wearing a bra. If that wasn't enough, I could see the bumps in her dress, where her nipples pushed against the silky fabric.

Sofia placed her soft hand against my chest. "You're shaking," she said.

I *was* shaking, from excitement. I had never been so aroused.

Sofia moved off the sofa to stand in front of me. She rested one knee on the sofa, next to me, and then moved her other leg until its knee also rested on the sofa, on the other side of me. She was straddling me with her long stockinged legs.

My heart pounded. I looked nervously towards the kitchen. "Maddie will be back soon," I said concerned.

Sofia put her fingertip on my lips. "Don't worry," she reassured me. "Victor will keep your wife busy."

I knew what that meant, of course. Victor was having his way with my wife, or at least trying to. But I wanted Sofia so much. Any lingering jealousy and concern I had for Victor with my wife disappeared as Sofia brought her hands to the edge of her dress, and then slowly—ever so slowly—pulled her dress up.

I almost came in my pants as Sofia's shapely, stocking-clad legs came into full view. Her dress was like a curtain, rising so my eyes could feast on her legs. Sofia raised her dress until I could see her heavy laced stocking tops, then her thighs above her stockings with the bare skin covered by only the straps of her garter belt. Sofia lingered there a moment, but finally she raised her dress more, letting me see her panties. Not the full coverage cotton panties my wife wore. But barely-there silk panties, a tiny triangle of sheer black lace with the wisp of a string on each side.

With her dress bundled around her waist, Sofia leaned over and kissed me. She explored my mouth with her hot tongue. "Unzip me," she begged. I found her zipper and pulled down, and then her bare breasts were before me. They were magnificent, large and full, yet so firm, capped by dark areolas surrounding eraser sized nipples. I squeezed and fondled her and sucked her hard nipples into my mouth.

Sofia moaned, and then reached between us and cupped my hard-on. "I've wanted to feel this since that first time we danced," she moaned into my ear. She unzipped me and pulled my cock out, and softly stroked me. I threw my head back, almost convulsing with the pleasure of Sofia's soft touch.

Suddenly I became aware of grunts and cries coming from the kitchen. It was Maddie's voice, and it sounded like she was in pain. "It's Maddie, she's hurt," I said, pulling away from Sofia.

"No, she's fine," Sofia assured me, urging me back onto the sofa. "Victor will take care of her, she'll enjoy it, you'll see."

"Are you sure?" I asked, but my concern for my wife ebbed away as Sofia teased my balls and stroked my shaft with her soft hands.

Maddie's cries turned to moans. Long soulful moans, moans that begged for more, moans of the type I have never before heard from my wife.

"See?" Sofia said smiling. "Victor is taking care of her. So we have time."

Then Sofia slid to her knees and took me into her mouth, and within moments I forgot all about my wife, in the kitchen, with Victor.

———◉———

I WOKE UP THE NEXT morning in the guest bedroom. At some point Sofia and I had moved there from the sofa. Sofia wasn't in bed and wasn't in the rest of the apartment either. I guessed she and Victor left earlier.

Sofia had been incredible. Her body was amazing, and so was her technique. She knew just want to do and when to do it to heighten my excitement and pleasure. She made me cum multiple times, more times than I thought possible in the span of just a few hours.

But in the clarity that always follows sexual satisfaction, my thoughts focused on my wife Maddie, not my new lover Sofia. Victor had fucked her. That was clear from all the moans and grunts I heard coming from our master bedroom and based on how long the moaning continued into the night, there was no doubt he fucked Maddie multiple times.

I made 2 mugs of coffee, and then opened the door to our bedroom. Maddie was awake, sitting up in the bed and looking blankly at the wall, as if in shock. She had her knees pulled up against her chest, and the blanket pulled to just below her chin. I handed her a mug and joined her in bed.

An awkward silence separated us. "Last night was crazy," I finally said.

Maddie nodded but didn't say anything.

"I got the impression they've done that before. I mean, seduced another couple."

Maddie nodded again, but still didn't say anything.

I remembered the cries I had heard the night before. I touched her arm. "Did he hurt you?"

She shook her head. "No, he didn't hurt me," she said softly.

"So ... you liked it?"

She hesitated, started to say something then stopped. Finally, she shrugged. "I don't know," she said, still looking at the wall. "It was different."

She looked at me. "Did you like it?"

I hesitated too, afraid the truth would hurt her feelings. "Like you said, it was different," I finally said.

Maddie studied me for long moments, and then nodded.

The phone rang. I picked it up and listened for a few minutes, and then hung up. "That was Victor. He said they had a great time last night. He invited us to their house next Saturday."

The thought of being with Sofia again got me hard. But I tried to hide my excitement.

Maddie looked at me. "Do you want to go?"

I shrugged and tried to keep my voice neutral. "One more time might be fun."

Maddie looked at me searchingly. "Well ... okay," she said, her voice soft and so low I could barely hear her. "One more time."

⚬

THE WEEK PASSED SLOWLY, as my anticipation for another evening with Sofia kept me constantly aroused. I fretted about Maddie with Victor again, but my consuming lust for Sofia help me bury my jealousy and concerns.

Victor and Sofia arrived. As always, Sofia looked luscious, showing plenty of cleavage and leg. She came to me and we kissed hello.

We chatted as we waited for Maddie to finish dressing. We joked about the costumes we were planning to wear at the upcoming Halloween party at the club. I told them I was thinking of dressing as Harry Potter, and I was trying to talk Maddie into dressing as a schoolgirl.

"Young schoolgirls turn you on, do they?" Sofia asked flirtatiously, coming to me and wrapping her arms around my waist. "You're such a bad boy. I love it." I grinned, wrapping my arms around her too.

Sofia's and my arms were still wrapped around each other when Maddie emerged from our bedroom. My jaw dropped when I saw her. She looked incredible. She wore a lycra black dress that clinged to her body. It ended around mid-thigh, and her long shapely legs were encased in sheer black hose. Sexy curly strands of her blonde hair framed her pretty face, and she wore bright red lipstick.

I was stunned. Could this sexy, alluring woman be my wife? I wanted to hold and kiss her, to make sure I wasn't dreaming. But I was still hugged to Sofia. Maddie hesitated as she took in the situation, seeing me with Sofia and Victor standing alone. Then she walked by me and went to Victor, kissing him hello.

We left our apartment and walked to the waiting limo. Before leaving the apartment we re-aligned ourselves to walk with our spouses, since people we knew were everywhere. As we walked to the limo I wanted to tell Maddie she looked gorgeous, but she seemed standoffish so I didn't get a chance.

Maddie and I sat together in the limo, and Victor and Sofia sat facing us. They poured champagne, and I clumsily spilled a little on my shirt.

"Oh, you poor thing, let me help you," Sofia cooed. She moved over to me and knelt on the thickly carpeted floor as she dabbed the spill with a napkin.

"Hey, I'm getting lonely over here," Victor said with a grin.

"It's okay Madison," Sofia assured Maddie as she rubbed my chest with the napkin. "I'll take good care of Adam."

Maddie smiled (although it looked to be forced), and then she joined Victor on the seat across from me. Sofia joined me on my seat and snuggled into my arm. Despite being so close to this former SI swimsuit model, I couldn't keep my eyes off my wife. I couldn't get over how stunning she looked. I had never seen her wear such a tight dress or show so much leg, and her legs looked more fabulous than ever in the sheer black hose.

My attention was drawn back to Sofia, as I felt her hand drop to my leg. She leaned into me and nuzzled my neck, as her hand moved up my leg, finally cupping my crotch.

Maddie watched as Sofia fondled me. I almost jumped when I felt Sofia rub me, and as always, her touch made me almost shudder with pleasure, but with Maddie sitting just across from us I tried to hide my pleasure, and instead I laughed nervously.

Maddie showed a hint of a frown. Looking into my eyes, she took Victor's hand and placed it on her thigh. That was all the encouragement Victor needed, and immediately he began caressing Maddie's thigh.

It was bad enough to see Victor's hand on my wife's thigh. But watching that large black hand moved up her leg towards the bottom of her dress was more than I could take. I was about to rescue my wife when Sofia slid between my legs. In what seemed like a single motion, she pulled out my cock and took me into her mouth.

It felt good to be inside Sofia's warm mouth, her tongue soft and probing. She was an expert at giving head. Despite what Victor was doing to my wife, I couldn't help but moan and roll my head back into the seat.

Sofia was amazing, working me to the brink of orgasm and then easing up, keeping me on the edge of cumming for long excruciating minutes. I panted as Sofia teased me, giving me slivers of pleasure while denying me the orgasm I craved.

I looked over to Victor and Maddie. I had almost forgotten about them. Victor's mouth covered Maddie's, and his hand was under her skirt. He pushed his hand against Maddie's thigh. Understanding what he wanted, Maddie uncrossed her legs. Victor moved his hand from Maddie's outer thigh to her inner and continued his upward journey, this time between my wife's legs, edging her dress higher and higher as he moved.

My eyes grew wide as I saw what Maddie wore under her dress. She was wearing *real* stockings, not pantyhose! And as Victor pushed her dress higher, I saw the stockings were attached to the straps of what surely was a garter belt! I couldn't believe it! Other than our wedding day, Maddie had never worn real stockings, much less a garter belt.

The sight of my wife in such sexy lingerie pushed me over the edge. I convulsed and shot my load into Sofia's mouth.

Victor's hand disappeared under Maddie's dress. Maddie moaned and arched her back, a clear signal Victor had reached her panties and was fingering her. Maddie writhed as Victor played with her. Victor moved Maddie's hand to his crotch. "Take me out and stroke me," he commanded.

Until that moment I hadn't noticed the huge tent formed in Victor's pants. Maddie unzipped him and reached inside.

"Easy, easy!" he exclaimed as she began pulling him out. Maddie tried again, being more careful and going slower, and this time she managed to pull him out.

My eyes grew wide at the sight of Victor's cock! He was huge, at least twice as long and thick as mine, with thick veins running up the sides and capped by a large bulbous head. There was no way my petite wife could get that huge monster inside her.

Seeming to read my mind, Victor grinned at me. "Don't worry Adam, she liked it last time. She had to get used to it, but by the end she was loving it, weren't you babe?"

But Maddie didn't answer. Instead, her body tensed as she orgasmed from Victor's finger fucking.

We arrived at Victor and Sofia's house (mansion better describes it). We had a drink and were about to separate into separate bedrooms when I pulled Victor aside.

"You know, we haven't talked about birth control," I said to him. In the spontaneity of our first swap, I didn't get a chance to tell him Maddie wasn't on any birth control.

Victor smiled and clapped me on the shoulder. "All taken care of, buddy, no need to worry." I smiled back. I had already assumed that, at his age, he had long ago gotten a vasectomy, but it was good to hear him confirm it.

We separated into different bedrooms. Once again Sofia was incredible, and I came multiple times. She didn't make me wear a condom, but I made sure to pull out, especially since she always welcomed my cum on her beautiful breasts and face.

———◉———

THE NEXT FEW DAYS WERE strained between me and Maddie. By unspoken agreement we didn't talk about what we did behind closed doors with Victor and Sofia. Seeing my wife with another man bothered me too much, and I sensed my being with another woman bothered Maddie as well.

I rationalized our swinging as a phase we were going through. We were still young, and it was good to get these things out of our system. But, as far as I was concerned, this phase of our marriage was over. I didn't want to swing anymore. The idea of my wife with another man made me too jealous, no matter how sexy and alluring Sophia was.

I asked Maddie when she bought the new dress and lingerie. Maddie told me Victor bought them for her, and sent them to her office. That made me furious. I didn't like another man buying my wife clothes and sending them to her behind my back. But I hid my anger, knowing I had no right to be mad given what I had done with Sofia.

Sofia was a jaw-dropping beauty; there was no doubt about that. But it was Maddie I kept thinking about. She had looked incredible in that tight black dress, and the recent memory of her shapely legs in the black thigh high stockings was etched in my mind. Maybe because we had been together so long, I forgot how sexy and pretty my wife was. Maybe instead of *asking* Maddie to wear tight skirts and garter belts, I should have *bought* them for her, and then she would have worn them for me, like she had for Victor.

Sofia was something else. A part of me – okay, a big part – still lusted over her. But having to share my wife with Victor was too high a price to pay. I decided to quit the country club and end our relationship with Victor and Sofia.

I left my office and took the elevator down to my car. We went down 5 floors, and then 3 people got in, two guys my age and a young schoolgirl. The girl wore a sweet pink bow in her long dark hair, and a school uniform, with a jacket over a crisp white blouse and a short, pleated skirt. The skirt was short, and the girl had shapely, long legs. She wore white knee high socks and classic saddle shoes. I felt guilty for ogling such a young girl, but I saw the other two men were salivating over her as well.

The 2 guys got off the elevator, leaving me alone with the young girl. Seeing only a partial profile, she looked to be 15 or 16. "Jailbait," I thought to myself, silently chuckling.

Then the girl turned to me, and my heart skipped a beat. It was Sofia!

She smiled at me. "Do you like?" she asked as she sweetly pirouetted on her tip toes. "You said you liked young schoolgirls, remember?"

I stood speechless. Sofia must have been in her mid-thirties, but with the pink bow in her hair and no make-up, she easily passed for a high school freshman or sophomore.

I looked at her again, my eyes moving from the pink bow in her hair, to the saddle shoes on her feet. She looked exactly like a schoolgirl returning home from school. But looking closer, I saw subtle differences. Her white blouse was conservatively buttoned almost to her neck, but the material was so light, I could see the lace of her white bra. Her skirt was shorter than what a real high schooler would wear, not even falling to mid-thigh. And she wore ultra sheer nude stockings. Were they pantyhose, or could she possibly be wearing a garter belt under such an innocent outfit?

"Oh, my shoe's come untied," she said, moving one leg in front of the other. "Can you tie it for me?"

As in a hypnotic dream, I pushed the HOLD button on the elevator, and then got on my knees and tied her shoe. As I did, she rubbed her calf against my cheek. The feel of her schoolgirl knee high socks against my skin sent shivers down my spine. I ran my hands over her newly tied saddle shoe, over her white knee-high sock, and then onto her knees, feeling the silkiness of the sheer nude nylons.

"You're a naughty man," she said in a schoolgirl voice as she pressed her stocking-clad thigh against my face. "You shouldn't be touching me like that."

I kissed her silky thigh, while my hands traveled up her shapely leg. She pressed the toe of her saddle shoe against my crotch, making me grimace with pain but also shudder with pleasure.

"What are you doing?" she said, feigning shock and fear as my hands passed the lacy tops of her stockings and moved to her bare thighs above. She *WAS* wearing thigh highs and a garter belt! Sofia rubbed my hard-on with the sole of her saddle shoe, the feel of the classic schoolgirl shoe being more erotic than the stiletto of a *Manolo Blanik* fuck-me-pump.

I pushed her skirt up to reveal lacy white panties that no doubt matched her bra. I saw with satisfaction that her panties were damp, her clit forming a camel toe in the soft material.

"No, no," Sofia protested as I pulled her panties aside and darted my tongue between the folds of her hairless pussy. "No, don't do that," she said as I pulled one of her shapely legs over my shoulder, opening her wider for my exploring tongue.

"No, stop touching me there, it's naughty," she moaned as I licked her clit. "No, it's bad, it's bad, you're a bad man," she protested as she cradled the back of my head with her hands and pulled me closer to her. Suddenly Sofia's body tensed, and I felt her shudder as an orgasm ripped through her body.

"You little slut," I sneered, enjoying this schoolgirl fantasy. "You liked that, didn't you? You liked my tongue on your clit. You liked it so much you came."

"No, no," Sofia said as she pretended to sob. "I've never done that before. I'm a virgin."

"Liar!" I hissed. I tore open her blouse, the little white buttons flying everywhere. I squeezed her large tits in my hands. "You're a little slut, a whore, you let all the boys touch you. Next you'll say you've never let anyone touch these before."

"I haven't!" she said, pretending to cry. "Stop, please, stop," she said, but through her bra I could feel her nipples stiffening.

I reached down and ripped off her panties. Then I lifted one of her legs up to my hip, at the same time unzipping my pants and pulling out by hard dick.

"No, no," Sofia begged, feeling my erection against her. "I'm saving myself for my husband. Please don't."

I shoved my cock into Sofia's wet pussy. My lust consumed me, like a wildfire burning unchecked through a field of dry grass. Sofia was magnificent! It felt like I was really fucking a schoolgirl! Fucking a virgin!

"Please, don't cum inside me," Sofia the young schoolgirl begged. "Don't make me pregnant. Please!"

"Then swallow my cum!" I said cruelly. I pulled out and roughly pushed Sofia to her knees, and forced my cock into her mouth. I gripped Sofia's silky dark hair as I savagely fucked her beautiful face, and when I came, I stayed deep inside her mouth, pressing her nose against my pubic hairs, forcing her to swallow all of my jism.

After I came, I staggered backwards, my fall stopped only by the elevator wall. It had been the best sex I had ever had. Ever. Nothing with Maddie came close.

Sofia stood up and giggled. "Wow, you *do* really like schoolgirls, don't you?"

Still panting, I looked down at her knees. Despite just cumming, I felt my lust returning. Sofia followed my eyes and smiled knowingly. She reached down and ran her fingertips along her knees.

She pouted. "You were so rough with me," she said, again in her schoolgirl voice. "You made me tear my stockings." She teasingly ran her unpainted schoolgirl nails along the runs. "Look how laddered they are, I won't be able to wear them again."

She pouted again. "Will you buy me new ones?"

I nodded, and she smiled. She reached down again and pulled up her white knee-high socks. They had gathered around her slim ankles during our fucking. I watched her and grew rock hard again.

She played with her blouse, which was ruined, its buttons still scattered on the floor. "Want me to wear this again?" she asked shyly, again like a schoolgirl.

I could only nod, my throat too dry to speak. She snuggled close to me and whispered in my ear, "I'll only wear it for you ... never for Victor."

"Do I fuck you better than Maddie?" she asked.

I didn't answer. But I knew the answer. Sophie did too, and she smiled knowingly.

Then she got on her knees and cradled by hard cock between the baby soft flesh of her large breasts. It flashed through my mind that Maddie had never given me a tit fucking; her breasts were too small.

Reading my mind, Sofia looked into my eyes as she tit fucked me. "Maddie can never give you what I can give you."

<hr>

A FEW DAYS LATER, VICTOR called and suggested a double date for the following weekend. I flinched when he said "*double* date," because I knew he meant Sofia with me, and Maddie with him. My wife dating another man? That bothered me. But my recent experience of fucking Sofia as an innocent schoolgirl still burned in my memory. I promised Victor I'd talk to Maddie.

That evening, Maddie reluctantly agreed to another evening with Victor and Sofia. I didn't say "double date" when I asked her because I didn't know how she'd take it. I got the feeling Maddie didn't really enjoy our new swinging lifestyle and was doing it for me. Maddie's reluctance made me feel guilty, but relieved too. Guilty, because I lusted so much for Sofia, and loved fucking her. And also guilty because I'd done something with Sophie she didn't know about.

Relieved, because knowing Maddie wasn't really into Victor, it made it easier for me to let Victor have her. I wanted Sophia, and the price was giving him Maddie. That seemed demented and wicked to me, but I guessed that was how the swinging lifestyle worked.

That Saturday we went to a nice restaurant with Victor and Sofia. While we shared a table, Sofia paired off with me and Maddie with Victor. It felt like a date, with Sofia snuggling up against me and whispering in my ear, and Victor with his arm around Maddie. I'm sure the waiter assumed Sofia was my wife, and Maddie Victor's. We would've had to do some serious explaining if any of our friends saw us, but the restaurant was in the next town, so there was little chance we'd run into anyone we knew.

"I've got an idea," Victor said later, as the valet fetched our cars. "Why don't you take Sofia to my house, and I'll take Maddie to yours? It'll give us more time to get to know each other."

"That's a great idea!" Sofia squealed with delight. "It'll be so much fun!"

My cock stiffened at the thought of having Sofia for the entire evening. Sofia's arm was around me, inside my coat, and she squeezed my ass. "It'll be fun," she repeated with a seductive smile.

I looked at my wife. Maddie didn't say anything, but her face was a mix of anxiousness and uncertainty. Under my coat, Sofia reached into my back pocket and caressed my ass, making me almost shiver with excitement.

"It might be fun," I said to Maddie, trying to keep my voice steady.

Maddie wore an "*I'm not sure about this*" expression on her face.

"It's just a few hours," I said, dismissing her unspoken concerns. "I'll be home before morning."

Maddie looked hurt, and she turned away from me. "Whatever," she said, a quiver in her voice like she was holding back crying. I felt bad, but my lust for Sofia consumed me.

Once again, sex with Sofia was amazing. I almost came in my pants when she took off her dress. She wore a black satin bustier, with garters that held up sheer black stockings. Her stiletto heels had to be at least 4 inches high. By 4am, I'd fucked her 3 times. I came once on her beautiful face, once on her magnificent breasts, and the last time inside her tight pussy.

I wondered if Sophia was on birth control. I'd never asked. I assumed she was because she had sex with other men. For a moment, I thought about how my life would change if I got Sophia pregnant. Maddie would be incredibly hurt and angry. I'm sure Victor would be pissed. Yet, a part of me would be proud to have a woman as magnificent as Sophia pregnant with my child. I forced myself not to think about this anymore, because I knew it was a betrayal of my wife.

Sofia fell asleep. With my lust satiated, the rational part of me returned. I felt terrible over how I treated Maddie earlier that evening. I got out of bed and dressed, being careful to not wake up Sofia. My plan was to get home early, bid Victor goodbye, and then apologize and make up with my wife.

Our apartment was dark and quiet, and I assumed Victor and Maddie were sleeping. I quietly approached the bedroom, not wanting to wake them up. A single lamp was on, but positioned as I was in the dark hallway, it was enough to illuminate the entire bedroom. What I saw took my breath away.

Maddie straddled Victor, who lay naked on the bed. They were fucking, Maddie's hands gripping his chest as she moved slowly up and down on his cock. When we had left our apartment earlier that evening, Maddie had worn her hair up. Now her long blonde hair fell loose off her shoulders and down her back, tangled blonde locks sexily framing her pretty face. My wife was nude, except for a garter belt and black stockings, and ankle strap high heels. Her dress, bra and panties lay on the floor.

Earlier that evening, I had noticed how sexy Maddie looked, but my attention had been focused on Sofia. Now, as I stood in the shadows watching them fuck, I couldn't get over how desirable my wife looked. Her long shapely legs looked so good in the stockings, and the sight of the garter straps pressing into her ass and thighs made my cock ache. I guess I had always taken Maddie's breasts for granted since they were small. But they were full and shapely, capped with hard perky nipples, and Victor couldn't seem to get enough of them as he cupped and fondled her.

Seeing my wife with another man was a punch to the gut. I wanted to pull Maddie off Victor. But I knew I couldn't do that, not after fucking Victor's wife. I had to suck it up and let them finish.

It's funny what draws your attention at times like this. What things burn into your memory. It wasn't so much Victor's cock moving in and out of Maddie's pussy. But the sparkle of her wedding and engagement rings as her left hand clutched his chest. Or the look on Maddie's sweet, pretty face, a mixture of pleasure and bliss, and her low intense moans hinting at ecstasy so immense to be almost religious. She enjoyed fucking Victor. He gave her pleasure, and she loved it. It sent a dagger through my heart, and I tried to remember if she had ever looked the same way with me. If she had ever made sounds with me, the way she was now with Victor.

I watched with masochistic fascination as Maddie slowly rose until only Victor's cockhead remained inside her, and then slowly lowered until fully impaled on his rod. She did this over and over, moaning with pleasure as she pulled up, and whimpering in discomfort as she pushed down, her pretty face initially contorted in a grimace of pain before transforming into a glow of pleasure and fulfillment.

Victor was big. He was so long, it seemed to take forever for Maddie to pull up, and even longer to push down. He was thick, too, and from my vantage point I saw my wife's pussy straining to accommodate his wide girth.

With a start, I realized Victor wasn't wearing a condom. Even though I knew he was fixed and clean, it bothered me that he was fucking my wife bareback. Was he going to cum inside her? I knew I was being hypocritical though because I had cum inside Sophia a number of times, including tonight. But I assumed Sophia was on the pill. I *knew* Maddie wasn't.

I also assumed Victor had a vasectomy but thinking back, I realized he never actually said that.

"Do you like fucking me, baby?" I heard Victor ask in a low guttural voice.

"Yeah ... yeah," Maddie said dreamily, her eyes half closed.

"You like my big fat cock?" Victor panted as their fucking became more frantic. I sensed they were both close to cumming. "Do you? Do you?"

"Yeah, yeah," Maddie moaned, her head falling forward and her long blonde hair whipping across Victor's broad black chest. "I like it, it feels so good."

"Do I fuck you better than your husband?" Victor hissed between pants. They were both close. "Am I better?"

"Ohhhh godddd," Maddie cried as she came, her orgasm ripping through her lithe body. "Better ... better ... and so much bigger. Ohhhh godddd ...."

As part of an upward thrust, Victor threw Maddie to the bed onto her back, and got on top of her, fucking her more savagely, pressing the wide girth of his hard cock against Maddie's clit to intensify the pleasure and length of her orgasm.

"Oh god, oh god," Maddie cried, wrapping her legs around Victor's waist, and digging the stilettos of her high heels into the back of his thighs.

Victor grunted and roared, and then lurched violently forward. I knew he was cumming inside my wife. He pushed deep inside Maddie and didn't pull out for what seemed like minutes, the muscles in his back and ass repeatedly convulsing as he shot what must have been gallons of his sperm inside my wife's womb. Even after he relaxed, signaling the end of his orgasm, he kept his cock planted deep inside my bride.

I staggered backwards in the darkened hallway, my knees weak, trying to process what I had just seen. Somehow, I managed to leave the apartment without being detected. I went down to my car to wait for Victor to leave.

***

MADDIE – AFTERMATH and Flashback

Maddie got into the shower. Victor had just left, and Adam would be home soon. As the hot water ran through her hair and sprayed her body, she reflected on the last three months, and how her life had changed.

Maddie shook her head in disbelief. She wasn't naïve. She knew some people swapped partners. She just never expected to be one of them. She and Adam were happy. Their sex life was satisfying, and they loved each other. She never thought they'd become one of those couples people whispered about.

She could imagine the hushed gossip at the country club. "You know Victor and Sofia swing, don't you? Oh yes, they swap partners, it's true, ask anyone. Well, have you noticed how much time Adam and Maddie are spending with Victor and Sofia? Do you think ... maybe ... they're a foursome?"

God, the country club. She wished they'd never joined. And she wished she'd never met Victor.

She remembered that first time at the club, when Adam introduced her to Victor. The memory made her shiver, even with the hot water jetting over her body. She had never met anyone like him, older but broad shouldered and ruggedly handsome, a man's man with the grace and charm of a diplomat, and so charismatic, with an intensity and presence so great it felt like a physical thing.

Maddie had never cheated on Adam, had never even considered it. But her attraction to Victor was immediate. After just a few minutes around him, her body tingled like never before, and her panties were wet. This had never happened to her before. No one had ever aroused her like this, so immensely, and so suddenly.

Yet, all would have been fine, if Adam would have stayed with her, not left her alone with Victor. But he was too interested in Sofia. Maddie couldn't refuse when Victor asked her to dance, not with Adam dancing with Sofia.

Victor danced wonderfully. So wonderfully, in fact, that she didn't notice as he gradually pulled her closer to him as they moved across the dance floor. Soon, her body was pressed against his. That's when Maddie felt his erection.

As a cheerleader in high school, Maddie was around the football team all the time. At practices, the boys wore tight stretch pants, just like the ones they wore during games, but without the pads. The pants were so tight you could see the outline of the boys' penises.

Maddie often glanced at the boys' crotches. Of course, she made sure no one ever caught her looking. It was harmless fun, and something she giggled about with the other cheerleaders.

For some boys, you couldn't see the outline of their penises. The cheerleaders giggled that those boys must have small ones.

For other boys—and this was usually the case with the black players—you could see their penises clearly outlined in the tight stretch pants. She remembered one black player—Clyde was his name—his penis seemed to go halfway down his thigh.

Her husband Adam was about normal size, compared to the men she had been with. Well, maybe a little smaller. Sometimes she wondered, a little guiltily, whether you'd be able to see the outline of his penis. if Adam wore the tight football pants,

Maddie remembered how it felt, pressed against Victor, his erection pressing against her stomach. He felt big, longer even than Clyde.

Victor wasn't crude; he didn't grind himself against her as they danced. But he didn't pull away either. As they danced and swayed, she felt his penis move and shift across her stomach, sometimes moving left and right, sometimes up and down. To her amazement, Victor got bigger and harder.

Maddie had felt light-headed and weak kneed, being in Victor's strong arms, in his commanding and charismatic presence, and with his hard penis pressed against her. And the fact that he was black ... the taboo of a white girl with a black man ....

The good wife part of her prayed for Adam to save her, to pull her away from Victor and take her back to the safe confides of their home and her lily white life. But the rest of her? She didn't know what the rest of her wanted.

"Let's go to the parlor," Maddie heard Victor say. "Less noise. We can talk."

Maddie looked anxious and uncertain. "I should wait here for Adam. He'll be looking for me."

Victor smiled a large reassuring smile. "Don't worry about that. Sofia will keep him company." Victor put his arm around Maddie and led her down the side of the ballroom and into the parlor. As he did, Maddie looked around the dance floor for Adam, but didn't see him. Victor closed the door.

Victor stroked Maddie's cheek. "You're lovely, so beautiful."

Maddie flushed, delighted by Victor's compliment, but uncomfortable and embarrassed. "No, I'm not," she said modestly, laughing nervously. "At least, not like Sofia. She's so beautiful, like a model. She has an amazing figure. I'm flat-chested compared to her." Maddie laughed nervously, trying to make it sound like a joke, but she felt like an idiot for rambling on.

Victor smiled reassuringly, and he touched Maddie's chin. Maddie froze and held her breath as Victor ran the tip of his finger along her neck and down her chest.

"You shouldn't ..." Maddie said as Victor's finger neared her breasts, her heart pounding in her chest.

"... please ..." Maddie whimpered as Victor's finger traced a circle around her breast.

"... I'm married ..." Maddie begged, a moan escaping her lips as Victor cupped and fondled her breast.

Victor raised an eyebrow, looking amused. He pulled his hand away.

"It's true," he said casually, his tone and expression showing no signs of his having just fondled her, "Sofia's breasts are large and wonderful. But I tell you—and I dare say most men would agree—shapeliness is just as important as size. And your breasts feel perfect to me. I'd love to see them someday."

Maddie blushed again, her heart pounding even harder. "Well, that's never going to happen," she said, laughing nervously. "I better go ... Adam's waiting for me."

"But, for me," Victor continued as if Maddie hadn't spoken, "I most admire a woman's legs. Long slim legs, toned and shapely. Just like yours."

Victor looked into Maddie's eyes. "Would it be too forward of me to say I'd love to see more of your wonderful legs? Why don't you raise your dress for me?"

"No, I don't think so," Maddie said, putting as much indignation into her voice as she could. She couldn't believe the nerve of this man. *Too forward of him?* He had just groped her, and he's worried about being too forward? She was married, how dare he?

Yet, why couldn't she bring herself to run away? He was so confident, so sure of himself. She had never met anyone like him. So powerful, so ... commanding.

Victor didn't say anything more, but his eyes never left Maddie's. Maddie felt herself wilting under his intense gaze. Flustered, she broke eye contact and looked away. Yet, she still felt Victor's eyes boring into her, silently commanding her to obey his demands.

It was like an out of body experience, with Maddie far above, watching herself. She watched as she reached down and, with shaky hands, clutched the material of her skirt, and slowly raised it.

"Very nice," Victor admired as Maddie raised her dress above her knees, and then past mid-thigh. "Your legs are even shapelier than I imagined. Don't stop, keep going."

Maddie flushed red, feeling a mixture of arousal and humiliation. How could she be doing this, exposing herself to this near stranger while her husband waited just in the next room? Why was she obeying this man? Why wasn't she running away?

"Keep going," Victor commanded. "Higher. That's it, keep going."

Maddie tensed as Victor reached out and cupped her pussy. "Well, isn't that a surprise," Victor said, amused. "You're damp."

Maddie's cheeks reddened even more; she had never felt so humiliated. She almost jumped when Victor ran a finger between her pussy lips, his touch sending waves of pleasure coursing her body.

Victor chuckled. "I think this is what they call a camel toe," he said, and then rubbed Maddie's clit through her panties and pantyhose.

"Ohhh goddd," Maddie whimpered as she tried, without success, to stifle a moan. She was so aroused, she was going to cum in just a few seconds if Victor kept fingering her. She knew she should pull away, push down her dress and run away, but she felt unable to move, frozen in place by Victor's charismatic and commanding presence.

"Your legs really are wonderful," Victor said almost casually as he continued to finger Maddie. "Wear shorter skirts, and higher heels. They'll look even better."

Maddie clutched Victor's arm and gritted her teeth. He was going to make her cum, it would only take another second ....

Victor abruptly pulled his hand away and Maddie gasped in frustration, whimpering at her unfulfilled orgasm.

Victor saw the longing in Maddie's pretty face and smiled. He flicked his hand dismissively. "You can go back to your husband now," he said, a look of amusement on his face.

For days after that first meeting with Victor, Maddie cursed herself for being so easily manipulated. My god, here she was, happily married, with Adam just in the other room, and she exposes herself to a stranger, and lets him fondle and finger her. Where was her good sense?

What was it about Victor? Why had she given in so easily to him? She knew she was attractive, and men still hit on her, even now after being married. She had never had problems fending off those men or been tempted by any of them. Why had she let Victor get so far?

The thought of Victor made her tingle. He had almost made her cum. She felt indignant at Victor's nerve, and angry at herself for her weakness. But also disappointment, because he pulled away before she climaxed. Feeling guilty, Maddie shook her head to get the thought out of her mind. She wanted to be a faithful wife, and wanting another man to finger her to orgasm was just as bad as sleeping with him.

Adam wanted to go to the next club mixer, and he gave her money to buy a new outfit. "You're so wonderful for going to these mixers with me," he had told her. "Here's some money—why don't you treat yourself to a new outfit?"

Maddie dreaded the thought of another club mixer, and the possibility of seeing Victor again. But networking at the club was important for Adam's job, so she reluctantly went to the mall to buy a new outfit. She browsed through the party dresses with the plunging necklines, and the skirts that were way too short. She knew Adam would love it if she wore sexy clothes like that. He was constantly encouraging her to dress sexier, but it just wasn't her. Growing up with two older brothers, she had always been a little tom-boyish, and felt more comfortable in jeans than dresses. She had never needed to dress sexy to attract guys. With her pretty face, silky blonde hair, and toned, athletic body, she never lacked for suitors.

Victor's words echoed in her head. "I want you to wear shorter skirts and higher heels." Remembering Victor's words made her shudder. He was so confident, so commanding, unlike any man she had ever known. Impulsively, Maddie quickly picked out a turtleneck, mini-skirt and high heels, and hurriedly paid for them before she lost her nerve.

At home and feeling nervous, Maddie tried on the new outfit. The clingy turtleneck molded itself around her breasts, and the tight mini-skirt ended around mid-thigh. She hadn't worn anything so short since her high school cheerleader outfit. The high heels weren't that high—only about 2 or 3 inches—but they were the highest she had ever owned, and she had to practice for over 30 minutes to walk without stumbling and looking foolish.

She looked in the mirror again and considered what jewelry to wear. Maybe the long pearl necklace Adam had given her as a wedding present. She imagined how pleased Victor would be when he saw the string of pearls dangling between her perky breasts.

Then, suddenly, she felt like crying, as the realization of what she was doing hit her like a physical blow. She had picked out the sexy outfit with Victor in mind, not her husband. Now she was picking out jewelry to please Victor, and she was even thinking of wearing the pearls Adam had given her on their wedding day. But not for Adam. For Victor. She sat on the edge of the bed, her guilt overwhelming. "What am I doing?" she asked herself.

Her eyes fell to her long legs. When she sat, the tight skirt hiked higher up her thighs so it ended just inches below her most private parts. She had lost her summer tan, so her legs had returned to their natural smooth lily white tone. Despite her guilty feelings, Maddie imagined how Victor's dark black hand would look against her white skin. She imagined Victor's hand on her knee, and moving up her thigh, moving under her skirt. She remembered how it felt when Victor cupped her pussy, his insistent fingers fingering along her slit and even touching her clitoris.

Maddie scooted up to lay on the bed. She covered her face with her hands. "What am I doing?" she asked herself again. Then, after long guilty moments, she gave into her body's desires, reaching down to pull up her new skirt, and then inserting her hand down her panties. "Oh god," she moaned as she rubbed circles around her clit. With her other hand she squeezed her breasts, and with her eyes clenched shut, she fantasized about Victor fingering and fondling her.

On Saturday, Maddie pulled out an old black dress to wear to the mixer. She wasn't going to give into Victor's demands. The new outfit was hidden in her closet. She planned to wear that for Adam sometime, when they went out alone.

After putting on her dress and pantyhose, Maddie stepped into her low heel pumps. She looked into the mirror and sighed. She remembered how fashionable all the girls dressed at the club. She went back into her closet and pulled out the new high heels, and slipped them on. She looked in the mirror, and noticed how the higher heels made her legs look even longer and shapelier. The dress buttoned up the front. She hesitated, then impulsively unbuttoned three of the lower buttons to reveal more of her legs, and then hurried out of the bedroom before losing her nerve.

"You look lovely," Victor said admiringly an hour later as he held Maddie's chair, his eyes on her legs. Maddie smiled reluctantly at the compliment, not entirely happy at the prospect of dining with Victor and Sofia. They had little choice but to share a table with the couple, given how welcoming they had been as she and Adam had entered the club.

Maddie did her best to hold down her skirt but, like any dress, it hiked up her legs as she sat. "Very nice," Victor said approvingly over Maddie's shoulder. He bent over so his lips almost touched her ear. "I don't think I've ever seen legs so shapely and alluring." Maddie blushed and looked away.

"Are those new heels?" Victor asked after sitting down. "You're so kind, to wear them for me."

Maddie flushed. "You think so much of yourself," she said sharply, hoping Victor wouldn't notice her redden cheeks. "Yes, for your information, they are new, but I bought them to wear for my husband."

"Of course you did," Victor said with a condescending smile. Then his tone turned serious and hard. "Next time I see you, I want you wearing a shorter skirt." His stare turned harder. "But not before then. For me only. Not for Adam."

Maddie looked indignant. "I'll wear what my *husband* wants me to wear, *when* he wants me to wear it," she said angrily.

Victor laughed, a cruel laugh. "Is that right? Then why do you wear dresses that hide your charms? Perhaps that's why Adam pays so much attention to Sofia."

Maddie frowned as she looked at Adam and Sofia. They were talking to each other, their heads close, completely oblivious to the rest of the world.

As if reading her mind, Victor smiled. "Don't mind them. The purpose of the club is to socialize, to form bonds and friendships. For example, take those two men over there." Victor gestured to the adjacent table. "Mark and Greg. I'm certain they'd love to get to know you better."

Maddie glanced to her right and saw two well-dressed men looking at her. They were older, well into their thirties, and looked like brokers or attorneys. They sat across from their gossiping, pleasantly plump wives. The Mark and Greg were checking Maddie out, spending a lot of time looking up and down her young body.

Maddie looked away quickly. She couldn't believe they were leering at her with their wives sitting so near. Victor leaned closer. Maddie shuddered as she felt his hot breath tickle her neck.

"You see, you're forming a new friendship with Mark and Greg," he whispered into her ear. "Now you need to bond with them. Cross your legs, and as you do, allow your dress to ride up your thighs."

Maddie looked disbelieving at Victor. "You can't be serious."

Victor smiled, but his eyes were intent and humorless. "Do as I say," he said in a low but commanding voice.

Maddie hesitated. But once again, she felt caught in Victor's spell, mesmerized, her will melting under this intense gaze. As if in a dream, she slowly crossed her legs. With Victor's command echoing in her head, she didn't try to stop her skirt as it parted where she had unbuttoned it, falling away to expose her shapely legs to mid-thigh.

"You see, that wasn't difficult, was it? Now then, let your high heel dangle from your toes."

"What?"

"You heard me," Victor said sharply.

Maddie inwardly sighed. Feeling silly, she gently flexed her foot, so the shoe fell off her heel, then dangling the high heel shoe from her toe. As she did, Victor kept an eye on Mark and Greg, and smiled.

"Very good, Madison. You have their full attention." Curious, Maddie surreptitiously glanced at the two men. To her surprise, they were both practically panting, their eyes ogling her legs.

Victor chuckled at the surprised look on Maddie's sweet, pretty face. "You didn't realize you're such a tease?"

"I'm not a tease," Maddie insisted.

"Perhaps not ... at least not yet. But it arouses you, doesn't it, to turn them on?"

"No, it doesn't," Maddie insisted. But she couldn't deny the tingling she felt in her panties. She felt ashamed and angry. "Why are you doing this?" she asked exasperated. "Why do you play these games?"

"Games?" Victor laughed dismissively. "Madison, making you expose your legs barely qualifies as a game. This, however ..." Victor reached over and placed his hand on Maddie's firm thigh.

"... this might be worthy of a game."

Maddie almost jumped as she felt Victor's hand on her leg. She looked down at her lap and almost shuddered at the sight of his large black hand on her thigh. It looked just like she had imagined in her fantasy. Jet black on lily white.

"Please, take your hand away ..." she whispered, stifling a moan as Victor caressed her inner thigh.

"Fingering you as Mark and Greg watch would be fun."

"... please stop ..." Maddie pleaded as Victor's fingers trailed up her leg and disappeared under her dress.

"I'm sure they would enjoy watching your beautiful face as you cum," he said.

"... my husband will see!"

Victor raised an eyebrow, looking amused. "I think Adam's attention is drawn elsewhere."

Maddie glanced at her husband and saw with a stab of jealousy that Victor was right. Adam seemed completely captivated by Sofia.

"In any case, no one can see except for Mark and Greg."

Maddie looked around nervously, and realized Victor was right. Due to the orientation of the room, only Mark and Greg could see underneath their side of the table.

"I want you to take your hand off me," Maddie said as sternly as she could, trying to keep her voice from shaking as Victor continued to caress her.

"Did you fantasize about me this week?" Victor asked as if Maddie hadn't spoken.

"What?"

"You heard me. Did you think about me while Adam made love to you? Did you fantasize about me while playing with yourself?"

"No, of course I didn't," Maddie lied, realizing she had replied too quickly. Victor smiled knowingly, and Maddie looked away, feeling like a little girl caught telling a lie.

"Madison, are you wet?"

"No, I'm not," Maddie said exasperated. "Now take—-"

Suddenly Victor's hand moved further up her skirt until his fingers touched her panties.

"You lied to me," Victor said scowling as he fingered Maddie's soaking panties. "Never lie to me, Madison."

"Stop!" Maddie gasped in an urgent whisper, covering Victor's hand with hers. She stole a glance at Mark and Greg. They both had huge tents in their pants, and Mark was even rubbing himself. Victor continued to finger her, pushing her towards an orgasm. She couldn't cum with Mark and Greg watching, it would be too humiliating.

"Please," Maddie begged, "I won't lie to you again, I promise, just stop."

Victor stopped fingering her but didn't pull his hand away. Smiling triumphantly, he eyed Mark and Greg. "They're wondering if your husband is going to let me have sex with you."

Maddie stared at Victor in horror. "You're crazy," she chided him. "Adam would never let you have me."

Victor smiled. "Are you sure?" he asked, gesturing across the table. "Are you sure he wouldn't give you to me, if I let him have Sofia? A trade – you for Sophia."

Maddie glanced across the table, her heart sinking as she saw Adam and Sophia laughing, their faces so close together to be almost touching. It was almost like Adam had forgotten she was there.

"Never," she insisted somewhat weakly, feeling less confident.

"You thought about me this week, didn't you? You wore your new shoes for me?"

"No," Maddie said, repeating her earlier denial. "Not for you. I wore them for my husband."

Victor shook his head. "Madison, I told you not to lie to me."

Maddie felt Victor move his fingers again, edging around the edge of her panties and pushing towards her clit. She abruptly pushed her chair back, the commotion causing Adam and Sofia to look up in surprise. "I ... ah ... I have to go to the ladies room," she said, hoping Adam wouldn't notice how flushed she looked.

Victor looked into Sofia's eyes. She smiled, as if understanding her husband's silent message.

"I'll go with you," she said cheerfully.

Maddie felt awkward and angry walking next to the woman who was so clearly trying to seduce her husband. Sofia seemed oblivious to Maddie's anger, taking Maddie's arm in hers and happily chatting like they were best friends.

"I know Victor's attracted to you," Sofia said. "I'm not surprised; you're so young and pretty."

Maddie pulled away, shocked at Sofia's bluntness.

"It's fine, really it is," Sofia said quickly, smiling reassuringly. "I don't mind. I just want to warn you." Sofia pulled Maddie close, smiling conspiratorially. "Don't let him do anal with you."

Maddie's eyes grew wide, her lips parting.

"At least not the first time," Sofia added quickly, pretending to misinterpret Maddie's shock as disappointment. "I mean, Victor's an incredible lover, you'll love it, he really knows how to please a woman. But he's so big. Huge! You'll want to get used to him before you let him up your bum." Sofia giggled like a schoolgirl, and affectionately squeezed Maddie's arm. "I love it, it feels so good, but I'm just warning you, you won't be able to walk right for a week."

Adam and Maddie had just gotten home when the phone rang. "It's Victor," Adam said to his wife. "He and Sofia are in the neighborhood and asked to stop by."

Maddie froze. She wasn't ready to see Victor again, not after the last time. That's why she wouldn't go to the club tonight but had instead insisted that they go out by themselves to dinner and a movie.

"We should invite them over," Adam said. "They're just down the street. We don't want to be rude."

Maddie started to protest, but she sensed her husband's excitement. She could tell he wanted to see Sofia again. Feeling hurt, she shrugged, and listened as Adam excitedly invited Victor and Sofia up to their apartment.

Maddie remembered Victor's command. "Next time I see you, I want you wearing a shorter skirt. But not before then."

Maddie had intended to wear the new outfit that evening with Adam—the turtleneck and mini-skirt. But at the last moment she had decided on a different skirt and blouse, and low-heel pumps. It wasn't because of Victor's command, she had told herself. She just felt more comfortable in less revealing clothes.

But now, with Victor on his way to see her? She didn't know what to do. Changing into a short skirt would be so humiliating. But Victor's words kept echoing in her head. "Next time I see you, I want you wearing a shorter skirt. But not before then. For me only. Not for Adam."

"I guess I better change," Maddie said with resignation. She saw the questioning look on Adam's face, and hurried into their bedroom before he could ask anything.

Maddie undressed, and hurriedly rummaged through her closet for the new outfit. She considered a moment, looking undecided, and then sprayed perfume between her breasts. She was about to put on the new outfit when she remembered an adult movie she had watched with Adam. Blushing and feeling embarrassed, she pulled down her pantyhose and panties to her knees, and spritzed a little perfume on her trimmed bush.

Maddie pulled her pantyhose and panties back on, then dressed quickly in the clingy turtleneck and mini-skirt. She also changed from the low-heel pumps she wore tonight to dinner and the movie, to her new higher heels that she wore last time at the club.

She brushed her blonde hair and checked her makeup, applying a fresh coat of lipstick. She was about to return when she hesitated, looking at the top of her dresser. While feeling guilty, she nevertheless snatched up the pearl necklace Adam had given her on their wedding day, and put it on around her neck, the string of pearls hanging between her perky breasts.

"You look great, honey," Adam said as she emerged from the bedroom. "Is that a new outfit?"

Maddie nodded hesitantly. "Um ... yeah. I had some money left over after buying these shoes. Do you like?"

Adam barely had time to nod before the door buzzed. Then Victor was standing in the door, smiling and leering at Maddie past Adam's shoulder. He looked her up and down, nodding appreciatively.

"I'll get drinks," Maddie said nervously, wilting under Victor's intense gaze. She retreated into the kitchen, hoping Victor wouldn't follow, but knowing he would.

Maddie was on her tiptoes and reaching for wine glasses when she felt Victor's presence behind her. "You smell delicious," he said as he nuzzled her neck, his face buried in her silky blonde hair. "You look incredible," he said as his hands worked under her turtleneck and felt her flat tummy. "Madison, you do have a wonderful body."

Maddie felt Victor's hands roaming under her turtleneck, moving towards her breasts. "Please," she pleaded in a low voice, putting her hands on Victor's and trying to push him away. "Adam's just in the other room."

Victor chuckled. "Let's see what they're doing," he said, and he guided Maddie to the doorway of the living room. Sofia was straddling Adam on the sofa, her dress pulled up around her waist. Maddie felt intensely jealous as she watched her husband reach behind Sofia and unzip her. She felt even worse as Adam's eyes grew wide at the sight of Sofia's braless breasts. Her breasts were perfect and so much larger than hers. And Maddie could tell they were natural. She barely stifled a sob as Adam fondled and sucked Sofia's nipples.

Suddenly, Maddie felt a hard, pulsing rod in her hand. Victor had pulled out his penis and was pressing it against her. Maddie tried to pull away, but Victor held her hand with his, making her hold his hard cock.

Despite seeing her husband with another woman, Maddie found herself fascinated by Victor's penis. It was long and thick and incredibly hard, like granite, with thick veins running up both sides of the shaft. And it was very black. It looked menacing, yet the skin was soft and unblemished. Her body tingled as she held him, and she felt almost dizzy with anticipation and excitement.

Maddie watched as Sofia reached down and cupped Adam's hard-on. "I've wanted to feel this since that first time we danced," Maddie heard Sofia say. Sofia unzipped Adam's pants and pulled out his penis. This was the penis Maddie was so familiar with, the only penis she had held, or sucked, or allowed inside her for almost 10 years. It was her husband's penis, the penis of the man she loved. But even as she watched another woman fondle and stroke Adam's penis, Maddie couldn't help comparing it to the one she held in her hand.

"Adam's is so small," Maddie thought.

Victor pulled Maddie back into the kitchen, easily lifting her onto the kitchen table. He pushed her skirt up around her waist. Maddie yelped when he tore her pantyhose from the waistband to her crotch, and yelped again when he ripped her panties off. Victor's brutal nature both frightened and aroused her.

Victor smiled and took a moment to appreciate the beauty of Maddie's pussy, hairless except for a thin landing strip above her clit. Maddie blushed as for the first time in almost ten years, a man other than her husband looked upon her most private parts.

Victor guided his cock to Maddie's pussy, rubbing the large bulbous cockhead between her wet pussy lips, and was satisfied when he heard Maddie moan. Maddie looked between her legs and saw the long, thick cock – the big black cock—that was about to penetrate her. It frightened her, it was so big. How could it ever fit inside her?

Victor held Maddie's hips as he slowly pushed his massive cockhead into the young blonde wife. "Ugh god, god!" Maddie cried at the violation. "It hurts!"

"Stop whining," Victor said dismissively. "You'll get used to it, and when you do, you'll beg me for it."

Maddie grimaced and bit her lip as, inch by inch, Victor penetrated her with this thick black cock. Perspiration fell off Victor's brow from the exertion. "Damn Madison, you're tight, as tight as a fucking virgin!" he growled.

"It hurts, it hurts," Maddie whimpered, tears flowing down her cheeks from the pain. She felt her pussy straining around Victor's rod; it felt as though she could feel the thick veins running up the sides of his cock. She looked between them, and her eyes grew wide. He still had at least six inches to push inside her! And he seemed to get thicker at the base! God, she already felt completely stuffed, how could she possibly fit all of him inside her?

Victor began pulling out and pushing back in, each time stuffing more cock meat inside her. Maddie grunted from the pain, her chest heaving, her hands frantically gripping the sides of the table.

But then, pleasure joined the pain, and Maddie's grunts turned into moans. Victor was so long and thick that he stimulated both her clit and g-spot with every thrust. The pleasure was incredible, its intensity magnified by the pain.

Suddenly Maddie tensed, her back arching as she came. It was like a dam rupturing, and she dug her manicured nails into Victor's back as tidal waves of pleasure cascaded through her body. She had never had an orgasm so intense, and it went on and on, never seeming to end. Then Victor grunted and his body tensed, and with a powerful lurch he also came, his cock pumping what seemed like gallons of his seed into Maddie's fertile womb. Her womb was unprotected too, because she wasn't on the pill.

They lay panting for long moments, their chests heaving in tandem. Maddie instinctively wrapped her arms around Victor's neck, and they lay there snuggling in the afterglow of their orgasms, his half-hard cock still inside her, her legs still wrapped around his waist.

"My god," Maddie thought silently, still panting but completely satisfied. She had never had better sex. She had never even *known* sex could be so good.

———⊙———

BACK TO REAL TIME

I felt disheartened as I sat in the car, waiting for Victor to leave. I felt paralyzed, in shock, my eyes focused on the door of the apartment building, trying to will the door to open and Victor to walk out.

The images ran through my head, of Maddie straddling Victor and her long blonde hair swaying across her shoulders as she moved up and down on his cock. I couldn't get over how sexy Maddie looked as she rode him, nude except for a garter belt, black stockings, and ankle strap high heels. Her choice of lingerie pained me as much as seeing them fuck. For years I had been after my wife to wear thigh highs and high heels, but she rarely did.

But she wore them for Victor.

Finally, the door opened, and Victor left. I waited a few minutes more, and then went up to our apartment.

"Hi," I said tentatively, seeing Maddie in bed. She looked freshly showered, and it looked like she had changed the sheets. I took off my clothes and moved to join her under the covers, but she stopped me.

"Could you take a shower first?" she gently asked, and I felt like an idiot. I had forgotten all about being with Sofia that night. The sight of Maddie with Victor had driven thoughts of Sofia from my mind.

"Sure, yes, of course," I said quickly, and I quickly hurried to the shower. I emerged a few minutes later, still toweling my hair. Maddie smiled and pulled back the covers, inviting me to join her.

"Did you have fun?" I asked.

"Yes, it was okay."

"*Just* okay?" I asked, raising an eyebrow. For some reason, I had an urgent need to find out how Maddie felt about Victor. Maybe I hoped she had faked those moans and orgasms, that she didn't enjoy fucking him as much as it looked. Or maybe the masochistic part of me wanted to hear my wife admit how much she adored getting pounded by the well-hung black man. I added, "Sofia told me Victor was really good in bed."

Maddie hesitated and looked away from me. "He is good, I guess," she said after a few moments.

"Sofia said Victor's hung like a horse." I laughed, trying to sound like I didn't care if he was or not. "So, is it true, bigger is better?"

"I don't know. It was different with him." Maddie frowned, and her tone became defensive, almost angry. "Why do you care?"

"Why do I care? Honey, you're my wife. We might be experimenting with swinging, but that doesn't mean I don't care about you, and how you're getting along with Victor. I mean, I know his penis is bigger than mine. I'm just wondering if that makes a difference, if it feels better."

Maddie's anger melted away. "Honey, he's not better than you," she said in a soft voice. She rubbed my arm affectionately, and reassuringly. "It's just different, that's all."

Maddie paused. "Is it better with Sofia?" she asked hesitantly, concern in her face. "She's so beautiful."

I took my wife into my arms. I said, "Honey, I'll admit, it's exciting to be with someone new. It's probably the same way for you, to be with Victor. But there's no one prettier than you."

Maddie beamed happily. "You liar," she said playfully, punching me. "Sofia's a model. She was in the *Sports Illustrated* swimsuit issue—twice!—and *Playboy* wanted her to be Miss January or July or something, but by then she had met Victor, and he wouldn't let her."

"What? I knew about the SI swimsuit issue, but not Playboy."

Maddie punched me again, harder this time. "You jerk!" she joked.

I laughed and took her again into my arms. "Honey, I don't care what Sofia was in, or almost in. You're way prettier than her, and sexier too."

Feeling a little surprised, I realized I meant it. I wasn't just saying it because Maddie was my wife. Yes, Sofia was beautiful and alluring. But Maddie had everything that Sofia had, *and* more.

Maddie's face was prettier than Sofia's, although this was probably debatable and depended on whether you liked blondes better than brunettes. Her body was just as firm, and her ass and legs were way better than Sofia's. Sofia had bigger breasts, but Maddie's were full and perfectly shaped, and there were lots of men (including me) who preferred girls with small breasts. Especially with Maddie's sweet blue eyes and blonde hair, her smallish breasts gave her an innocent, college coed (or even barely legal) look.

Maddie was blessed with better raw material than Sofia. If Maddie tried, she could blow Sofia away in looks and sexiness. I wondered if Victor knew that. Maybe he saw beyond Maddie's scant use of makeup and near-shapeless clothing and recognized her potential to be something really special.

The thought upset me. It took Maddie having sex with another man for me to fully appreciate her beauty and sexiness. I got on top of my wife, intent on correcting my mistake.

"Honey, you're so pretty, much sexier than Sofia," I said as I pushed my hard cock into her pussy. She welcomed me, opening her legs and wrapping her arms around me. But despite my renewed passion for my wife, I started softening. Maddie's pussy wasn't as tight as usual, which wasn't a surprise since she had just fucked Victor who knows how many times. There wasn't enough friction to keep me hard, and Maddie also didn't seem to be enjoying it much.

Concern spread through me, as I wondered if I'd ever get my wife's tight pussy back. I thought again at how Victor's enormous cock stretched Maddie's pussy so much. Would her pussy ever return to normal, the way it used to be, where it fit my penis like a snug silky glove?

I was surprised to realize I was hard again. But why? I could still barely feel the walls of Maddie's pussy. So, what happened to get me excited? Suddenly, I realized the more I thought about Victor fucking Maddie, the harder I got. The more I thought about Victor's big black cock stretching and loosening her pussy – maybe permanently – the harder I got.

A mixture of jealousy and arousal flooded over me. I didn't want to think about Maddie getting banged by Victor with his massive black cock. But the more I thought about it, the more aroused I became. I closed my eyes and allowed the memories of not too long ago to playback in my head. I remembered how Maddie had wrapped her stocking-clad legs around Victor, and how she dug her stiletto heels into the back of his thighs to urge him deeper inside her. Within moments I came, my sperm joining Victor's that he had deposited in Maddie earlier that evening.

———— ❦ ————

I'M NOT ONE OF THOSE guys who fantasize about his wife getting fucked by other men. Wife watching and cuckold fantasies had never turned me on before. But over the next week I couldn't get the images of Maddie and Victor out of my head. I had a constant hard-on, and I even masturbated a few times in the bathroom at work.

It wasn't just the images, it was also what they had said.

"You like my big fat cock? Do you? Do you?"

"Yeah, yeah, I like it, it feels so good."

"Do I fuck you better than your husband? Am I better?"

"Ohhhh godddd. Better ... better ... and so much bigger!"

The memories hurt and left me jealous and insecure. But somehow, those feelings intensified my arousal, like throwing gasoline onto a fire.

They frightened me, too. I had ventured into this wife swapping lifestyle so I could bed Sofia. Now, though, my interest was shifting from Sofia to Victor and Maddie. The thought of them together got me hard. But did I want to risk letting Victor get his hands on Maddie again? What if she got addicted to his big black cock? Was I somehow a closet gay, getting off on seeing huge black cocks fucking petite blonde pussy? All these thoughts were disturbing and upset me. Yet, whenever I thought about it—thought about Victor fucking my wife—I got hard and masturbated to a ferocious orgasm.

"Victor called me today," I said to Maddie a few days later. I had considered not saying anything but knew Maddie would eventually find out. "He wanted to know if we planned to be at the club this weekend."

"What did you say?"

"I said I'd get back to him. Do you want to go?"

Maddie hesitated. It seemed like she was picking her words carefully. "I guess we have to," she finally said. "Don't you need to network with these people for your job?"

"Yes, but I've been thinking ... maybe the club isn't the best thing for us. This thing we've been doing with Victor and Sofia. Maybe we should stop. What do you think?"

"Well, I don't know," Maddie replied noncommittally. "Sofia invited me to lunch tomorrow."

"She did?" I said with surprise.

"I'm sorry, she called today, and I forgot to tell you. Anyways, it might be a little awkward if we don't go to the club after she takes me to lunch tomorrow."

"Yeah, I guess," I said.

I searched Maddie's face. Her tone was still neutral, but I sensed a little – what was it? Apprehension? Was she afraid I'd say no about going to the club? Was she concerned I'd say no to her sleeping with Victor again?

I finally said, "Well, then, I guess we better go. I'll call Victor and let him know we'll be there."

"Okay, if you think that's best," Maddie said, shrugging nonchalantly, acting like she didn't care either way. Yet, did her face show relief, maybe even excitement, that she would be seeing Victor again?

⚬

MADDIE FIDGETED NERVOUSLY as she waited for Sofia to arrive. She dreaded lunch with Sofia. It wasn't like she was going to lunch with a girlfriend, or even a casual acquaintance. She had slept with Sofia's husband! Was Sofia planning on confronting her, telling her to stay away from Victor? God, why had she ever agreed to this lunch? But she couldn't really say no, and Sofia had been so nice to her over the phone.

"Oh Maddie, I'm so sorry for being late," Sofia said a few minutes later. She hugged Maddie and kissed her on the cheek. "Traffic was terrible. But I'm so happy to see you!"

Maddie's apprehension diminished as they sipped wine and gossiped about people at the club. Soon they were giggling like school girls and acting like best friends.

Sofia leaned back in her chair and her eyes drifted to below the table. "Maddie, you really should wear shorter skirts," she admonished in a playful, motherly voice. "Your legs are so nice, you should show them off."

Maddie giggled. "Oh my god, you sound like Victor." Then she realized what she said, and brought her hand to her mouth, horrified. "I'm sorry, that was so insensitive, I wasn't thinking—"

Sofia smiled. "Maddie, it's okay," she said reassuringly. "I don't mind you're sleeping with my husband. This is something we do, we have an open marriage. It's fun, exciting, to play with other people. Variety is the spice of life. The club is really a wonderful place for that."

"Really?"

"Oh, absolutely. Everyone is really fit and good looking. Well, most people anyway. And many are open to having some harmless fun." Sofia looked quizzically at Maddie. "Have any other men approached you yet?"

Maddie looked taken aback, shocked. "No!" she said quickly.

Sofia laughed and squeezed Maddie's hand affectionately. "It's okay, honey, let yourself have fun. I'm sure Adam won't mind—he seems to like swinging. In fact, Victor will probably be more jealous than Adam. My husband's really taken with you."

Maddie was speechless. She hadn't considered being with other people. She was still trying to get use to the idea of her extramarital activities with Victor. "Well, no one's shown any interest in me," she said, not knowing what else to say.

"Oh Maddie," Sofia said, amused. "There's a lot of interest in you. A lot. From many men at the club."

Maddie blushed. Were people talking about her at the club, openly talking about her affair with Victor, wondering who would bed her next? She felt like a piece of meat, and practically shuddered at the thought. It was demeaning, but – she had to admit – thrilling too.

Suddenly Maddie felt Sofia's hand on her thigh. "You believe me, don't you? You're so young and pretty, and you have such a cute figure. Lots of people would like to get to know you better. And not just men."

Maddie turned scarlet. "Um, well," she stammered, feeling Sofia's caresses on her bare thigh.

Sofia giggled at Maddie's obvious discomfort and pulled her hand away. "Don't worry, I won't rape you," she said with a twinkle in her eye. "But sometimes, Victor and I like to share a pretty girl. You'll think about it, won't you? I promise you'll like it."

"Um, sure, I guess," Maddie stammered, feeling more awkward than she had ever felt in her life.

Sofia squeezed Maddie's hand reassuringly. "Maddie, you should listen to Victor, you really should. Wear shorter skirts. Your legs are so nice. Dress sexier at the club, and flirt more. You'll have so much fun teasing all the boys, you really will."

"Um, okay." Then Maddie realized Sofia hadn't mentioned Adam. "Do you hear people talking about Adam?"

"Oh, don't worry about Adam," Sofia said almost dismissively. "I told you, the people in the club are fun. And they're fair. There'll be a lot of wives who'll sleep with Adam, so their husbands can sleep with you."

Maddie slowly leaned back in her chair, feeling shocked. "Do you mean—did Victor force you to sleep with Adam, so he could sleep with me?"

Sofia looked shocked. "He didn't force me, of course not. I like Adam, he's sweet. I'm just saying, in a good marriage where both spouses are open minded and like to have fun, sometimes the wife will sleep with someone she might not otherwise, so her husband can sleep with the girl he wants. And sometimes it's the other way around."

"So ... you mean, you wouldn't have slept with Adam, if Victor hadn't wanted to sleep with me?"

Sofia grimaced. "That makes it sound so bad. I like Adam, I really do. He's just not my type."

"Well, um ... what *is* your type?"

Sofia smiled mischievously. "Honey, I think you know my type. And, from what Victor tells me, you like the same type. I mean, I'm not *obsessed* about size. I've enjoyed playing with many men who aren't as big as Victor. I mean, hardly *anyone's* as big as my husband. But Adam—he's really small, isn't he?"

"No he's not!" Maddie said, immediately coming to the defense of her husband.

"Oh, okay," Sofia said, backing off quickly upon hearing the anger and indignation in Maddie's voice. "I'm sorry, I didn't mean to offend you. It's just ... well, I had assumed that's why you and Adam were getting into swinging. He was letting you experience men with—you know—men who were better endowed."

"No, that's not why. We just thought ... I don't know ... I guess we thought it might be fun to experiment with other people for a while."

"Oh, well, that's understandable." Sofia was quiet for a moment, and then her curiosity got the better of her. "So ... size doesn't make a difference to you?"

Maddie crossed her arms defiantly. "It doesn't make a difference for most women," she said, remembering things she had read in magazines.

Sofia seemed to read Maddie's thoughts. "Women say that, I know, but—well—it didn't feel different being with Victor? Compared to Adam?"

"Well, of course it felt different!" Maddie said without thinking, exasperated. "Your husband's as big as a horse!"

Maddie scowled at Sofia, and then realized the outrageousness of what she had just said. The two girls looked into each other's eyes, and then broke out laughing, the tension between then immediately easing. They laughed so long their stomachs ached.

Tipsy from wine and still feeling silly from laughing so hard, Maddie's curiosity got the better of her. She asked, "So, do you really think Adam's that small? I mean, compared to other men you've been with?"

Sofia didn't answer. Instead, she squeezed Maddie's hand and smiled caringly, a sympathetic look on her face.

⚬

MADDIE TIGHTLY CLUTCHED Adam's hand as they entered the club. She was wearing the Lycra dress again, the one Victor had sent her a few weeks ago, just before she and Adam visited them at their mansion. The dress was so revealing she almost hadn't worn it then, and that was back when only Victor and Adam were going to see her in it. Now, lots of men were going to see her in the dress, and butterflies flittered through her stomach as she nervously held onto her husband's arm.

Maddie felt every male head turn as she walked by. She blushed, feeling like a piece of meat on display. Did they know about her affair with Victor? Maddie remembered what Sofia had said. "There's a lot of interest in you, a lot." Did these men think she was available? Were they hoping to sleep with her? Maddie nervously glanced around. Many of the men were hungrily leering at her. She clutched Adam's arm even tighter.

"There you are, I've been looking for you two." Adam and Maddie turned and saw a smiling Sofia approaching. Maddie was relieved to see her friend. Sofia hugged Adam and kissed him hello on the cheek. Maddie felt a twinge of jealousy, but she knew it was silly to feel that way given the situation. Then Sofia linked her arm with Maddie's. "Honey, come with me to the ladies room," she said cheerily.

"You look so good!" Sofia gushed enthusiastically, eyeing Maddie up and down after closing the bathroom door. "I wish my legs were as long and slim as yours, I'm so envious."

"Oh stop that, your legs are fantastic," Maddie said, glancing down at Sofia's legs. Sofia wore a mini-dress that showed even more leg than Maddie's, and her legs were encased in black hose, just like Maddie. Even while returning the compliment, Maddie knew that Sofia was right, her legs *were* nicer. The realization made her feel proud, but then she felt guilty and catty. "Anyways, your breasts are so much bigger than mine," Maddie quickly added, the admission easing her guilt.

Sofia beamed and gave Maddie a hug. "Size isn't everything, honey," Sofia said. Then both girls remembered their last conversation about penis size and giggled. Even while laughing, Maddie felt guilty, knowing part of the joke involved Adam's size. Sofia sensed the sudden cloud over Maddie's mood and frowned. "Honey, you need to learn how to relax and have fun."

Maddie shrugged, uncertain what Sofia meant. "I wore this dress," she said, motioning to herself. While walking to the bathroom, the static cling of the Lycra against her stockings caused her dress to hike up her legs. "It's so short, I'm afraid people will see my stocking tops," Maddie said, tugging down her dress.

Sofia laughed. "Honey, everyone already knows you're wearing stockings! The dress is so tight you can see the bumps of your garter belt."

Maddie looked down and was horrified to see that Sofia was right. How hadn't she noticed this before? "Oh my god, I can't go out like this," she said anxiously.

Sofia squeezed Maddie's arm reassuringly. "Honey, this is what I mean, you worry too much. Anyway, men like seeing garter bumps, you'll have them eating out of your hand. Just remember, whenever you wear a clingy dress like this, you're on display. Dresses like this don't hide much. Men will know you're wearing a bra, too. They'll be able to see your bra strap as easily as I can."

"Oh," Maddie said, feeling foolish. She wasn't used to wearing tight, sexy clothes like this. "So ... are there different bras I should wear?"

Sofia giggled. "No, silly. You shouldn't wear a bra at all."

"I can't do that," Maddie said warily. "The material is so thin."

"Of course you can. I'm not wearing a bra, and neither are most of the girls out there tonight." Without asking for permission, Sofia unzipped Maddie's dress. In one quick motion, she unsnapped the back clasp of Maddie's strapless bra, and pulled it away. Then Sofia re-zipped Maddie's dress. Both girls looked into the mirror. The clingy fabric of the Lycra dress molded itself around Maddie's small breasts. "You look lovely," Sofia said admiringly, unable to take her eyes off Maddie's perfectly shaped mounds. "Your breasts are so firm and perky, you don't need a bra." With a laugh, she added, "My breasts are bigger, but no one would call them perky."

Maddie looked doubtful. "But the material's so thin—"

"—that people might be able to see your nipples, if you get aroused?" Sofia said, completing Maddie's sentence. "Let's check."

Sofia stepped back so she stood directly behind Maddie. Sofia was taller than Maddie, so she easily looked into the mirror over Maddie's shoulder. Before she could protest, Sofia moved her hands to Maddie's chest and cupped her friend's breasts. "You're so firm," Sofia cooed as she fondled Maddie's tits. She easily found Maddie's nipples through the stretchy Lycra material and rubbed them between her thumbs and fingers. "Oh my, your nipples get so hard."

Maddie didn't know what to do. Looking in the mirror, she watched as Sofia fondled her. She couldn't help moaning as Sofia rubbed her ultra-sensitive nipples. She felt unsteady on her feet and reached back to steady herself. In doing so she clutched Sofia's thigh and felt the garter belt strap through the fabric of the older woman's mini-dress. Maddie reflexively pulled her hand away, but Sofia grasped Maddie's hand and brought it back to her thigh.

"It's alright honey, I won't bite." Sofia pulled up her skirt so Maddie's hand was on her lacy stocking top. Then Sofia covered Maddie's hand with hers and slid Maddie's hand until it rested on her garter strap. Maddie couldn't believe how soft Sofia's naked skin felt above her stockings, and without thinking began caressing her friend's thigh. "Oh yes honey, that feels good," Sofia breathed into Maddie's ear.

Maddie came to her senses. She detached herself from Sophia and hurried from the bathroom, feeling unsteady in her high heels. The club had gotten crowded. She looked for Adam but didn't see him. Confused and needing to settle her nerves, she went to the bar and ordered a white wine. She gulped it down quickly, and ordered another.

"Party girl, that's what I like," Maddie heard someone say behind her. She turned and saw it was Mark. She blushed, remembering how she had teased him a few weeks back.

"Don't stop on my account," Mark said, a big grin on his face as he motioned to her wine glass. "I like a girl who knows how to have fun."

"I was just thirsty," Maddie said, knowing how feeble her excuse sounded even as she said it. She turned back to the bar, hoping Mark would go away.

Instead, Mark offered his hand. "We've never been formally introduced. I'm Mark."

Maddie reluctantly swiveled to face Mark, and politely smiled. "I'm Maddie," she said, briefly grasping Mark's offered hand.

"You and your husband – Adam, right? – you hang around with Victor and Sofia a lot."

Maddie blushed again. "Sometimes we do," she said evasively. Did Mark know? Maddie noticed that Mark watched her lips as she spoke, not her face.

"So ... do you guys get together outside the club, too?"

"Well, sometimes," Maddie stammered, her discomfort magnified as Mark kept his eyes focused on her mouth. "Is it any of your business?" she asked defiantly.

Mark laughed, looking amused. "Don't get upset. I'm just making conversation."

"I'm not getting upset," Maddie said defensively. She didn't like this man. Maddie judged him to be a rich lawyer with family money, a person used to getting whatever he wanted.

Mark smiled and moved closer so only Maddie could hear. "So, are you giving us another show tonight?"

Maddie looked bewildered. "Show? What do you mean?"

"Come on," Mark said in a condescending voice. "I know your type. You like to show off your body."

"I do not!" Maddie said indignantly.

Mark looked at Maddie knowingly, and she blushed, remembering again how she had exposed her legs to him a few weeks ago. He sniggered mockingly as he saw Maddie's obvious discomfort, humiliating her even more. He took a step back and looked Maddie up and down. His hungry eyes focused on her bosom. "That dress shows you off well. Nice choice."

Maddie flushed under Mark's leering gaze. She knew she was showing off a lot in the dress. The dress barely reached her mid-thigh. To her horror, she realized her nipples were still erect and outlined through the thin stretching material. She wondered where Adam was. She wished he'd come and save her from this brute.

"Listen, you don't need to play games with me. I know you're swinging with Victor and Sofia. My wife's nothing much to look at." Mark gestured over his shoulder, and Maddie saw a woman sitting across the room, chatting with other girls. His wife (her name was Suzanne) was cute, but overweight.

Then Maddie felt Mark's hand on her knee. She looked back at him. He was so close his lips almost touched her cheek. "I hear your husband's trying to do some business. I'm well connected. I can introduce him to the right people." Mark edged the tips of his fingers under Maddie's dress. "Provided, of course, I get what I want."

Maddie couldn't believe Mark's blatant proposition. "No thank you!" Maddie said coldly, putting as much indignation into her voice as she could. She pushed Mark's hand away and slid off the stool. But as she did, her skirt hiked up exposing her stocking tops and garter straps.

Mark grinned at the sight. "Thanks babe, now I'll have something to fantasize about when I'm fucking Suz tonight."

Maddie blushed deep red. She hadn't meant to flash Mark, but it was clear he thought she had done it on purpose. Worse, Mark's wife had seen what had happened, and was walking quickly towards her.

Suzanne grabbed Maddie's arm. "I saw what you did, bitch! You stay away from my husband!"

"I'm sorry, I'm sure you're mistaken. We were just talking." Maddie tried to pull her arm away, but the larger woman was too strong. She glanced around the room, hoping to spot Adam, hoping he would help her. *Where was he?*

"Don't lie to me, bitch!" Suzanne hissed angrily. She was practically shouting, and people were turning to look. "I've heard about you! I've heard about the games you play! Flaunting your body, using your looks to seduce men!"

Maddie saw that everyone had turned to look at her. She flushed red, feeling even more exposed in her revealing dress. "Please," Maddie pleaded in a low voice. "This is all a mistake. We were just talking."

"A mistake?" Suzanne mocked. She, too, had noticed the crowd around them. She intended to do everything she could to embarrass and humiliate the blonde slut. "Look at you! Your dress is practically see-through. Are you telling me you're not trying to expose yourself? You're a slutty exhibitionist! I saw you pull up your dress, exposing yourself to my husband!"

"No, it was an accident, I didn't do it on purpose," Maddie pleaded, tears falling down her cheeks. *Where was Adam?* She needed him to save her from this!

"So, you admit you exposed yourself to my husband. You slut! You look like a hooker, you should be walking the streets."

Suddenly Suzanne grabbed Maddie's long blonde hair, making Maddie yelp in pain. Suzanne jerked Maddie towards her, so their faces almost touched. "Stay away from my husband!" Suzanne growled. "Or I swear to god, I'll hurt you! I'll cut off all your pretty hair, that's what I'll do! I'll crew cut you!"

"Suzanne, let her go!" a stern voice commanded. *Thank god, Adam is finally here,* Maddie thought.

But when Suzanne let go, Maddie saw it wasn't Adam. It was Victor.

Victor scowled into Suzanne's face. "The bitch made a pass at Mark," Suzanne said, her arms crossed defiantly.

Victor glared at Mark, his muscular body towering over the smaller man. Mark took a step back, a wary look on his face. He was clearly intimidated by the large black man. The swagger Mark had shown just a few minutes before with Maddie had vanished in the presence of the dominating Victor.

"Come on honey," Mark said conciliatorily to Suzanne. "Maddie didn't come on to me. It's all a misunderstanding."

Suzanne scowled at her husband. "*Whatever*," she finally said. She grabbed Mark's hand and pulled him away, casting a final deadly glare at Maddie before disappearing into the crowd.

Maddie wiped away her tears and forced herself to stop crying. Feeling embarrassed and completely humiliated, she quickly walked away in the direction *opposite* to Suzanne and Mark. The crowd parted to let her through, but all eyes were on her, and the room was full of gleeful murmuring and snickers. Maddie tried not to listen to the cruel things people were saying as she walked by. Just wanting to get away, she entered an empty parlor off the ballroom. She collapsed into a chair and started sobbing uncontrollably.

After a few minutes she heard the door open. She felt comforting hands on her shoulders. "*Finally, Adam is here*," she sighed to herself in relief. But when she turned her head, it wasn't Adam.

Again, it was Victor.

Victor hugged Maddie into his arms. "I know you're upset. Don't be. Suzanne is a fat bitch, and her husband Mark is a lazy asshole. They live off family money. You're way better than them."

"She called me a slut!" Maddie cried, tears streaming down her face. "She said I looked like a prostitute!"

Victor kissed away Maddie's tears. "She's jealous, that's all. She hates you because you're beautiful and sexy." Victor hugged Maddie tighter, and he continued to kiss away the tears on her cheek. "You're everything she isn't."

Maddie leaned into Victor. It felt good to be in his strong arms, pressed against his muscular chest. She felt safe and secure. Victor's lips moved from her cheeks to her mouth. When he kissed her, she didn't stop him.

————◆————

ADAM FOLLOWED MADDIE and Sophie as they walked to the ladies room together. He found an inconspicuous spot around the corner and watched the door to the ladies room, anxiously waiting for his wife to emerge.

He couldn't believe how hot she looked, the tight black dress exposing her wonderful legs to mid-thigh, and her shapely legs encased in sheer black stockings. He knew she was wearing a garter belt from the telltale bumps, even before fondling her in the car as they drove to the club. He hadn't wanted to go to the club after seeing what she was wearing. He wanted to jump her right then and fuck all night. But he had already told Victor they would be coming to the club.

Adam's heart leaped when the door opened and Maddie walked out, followed a few seconds later by Sofia. He moved towards her, and then paused. Something appeared wrong. Maddie looked flushed and had a confused look on her face. Sofia had an odd expression on her face, too. Disappointment? Unsatisfied arousal? He got hard imagining what might have happened in the bathroom. His curiosity got the better of him, so instead of joining Maddie, he hid in the crowd, watching her.

Adam watched as Maddie walked to the bar and ordered wine. Things became more interesting when a man approached her (Adam had heard his name was Mark). It was clear Mark was hitting on Maddie. Adam was about to join his wife and save her from Mark's advances when he felt someone press against his back.

"Hi there handsome," said a sultry voice. Adam turned. It was Sofia.

Sofia looked past Adam's shoulder, at the bar. "Looks like Mark is hoping to get lucky tonight with your pretty wife," Sofia said in a playful voice.

"I need to get over there," Adam said.

"No, you don't," Sofia said mischievously as she grabbed Adam's shirt under his jacket. She teasingly ran her manicured nails over his back. "Let's see what happens."

Just then, Mark placed his hand on Maddie's knee. Sofia sensed the sexual tension building in Adam's body as they watched Mark caress Maddie's thigh and edge his fingertips under her dress.

"This excites you, doesn't it?" Sofia whispered into Adam's ear. "Watching as another man seduces your wife?"

They watched as Maddie pushed Mark's hand away, and then slid off the bar stool. Sofia felt Adam's breath catch in his throat as Maddie's dress rode high up her leg, exposing her stocking tops and garter belt. Sofia smiled. "Nice move," she whispered approvingly. "Your sweet wife is learning."

Adam looked sharply at Sophia. Maddie flashed Mark on purpose?

At that moment, Suzanne grabbed Maddie's arm and started screaming at her. Alarmed, Adam took a step towards his wife to save her, but Sofia again pulled him back. "She's fine," she said reassuringly. "Over there, see? Victor is coming. He knows Mark and Suzanne better than you. He'll handle it."

Victor quickly diffused the situation, in the process humiliating Suzanne and Mark. Suzanne angrily stomped away, followed closely by an emasculated Mark. Looking distraught, Maddie hurried away in the opposite direction. Laughter and whispered gossip followed her as she disappeared into the east parlor, her face red with embarrassment and shame.

"Look," Sofia said, gesturing at Victor who was moving unnoticed in the opposite direction. "He's going the back way to the east parlor." She tugged Adam's arm excitedly. Like a giddy schoolgirl, she said, "Come on, let's go see."

Sofia led Adam to the hallway Victor had taken. It led away from the crowd, so they (like Victor) were unnoticed. They approached the door to the east parlor, but instead of going in, Sofia pulled him into the room next door.

"Not many people know about this," Sofia explained as she pulled back curtains that covered one of the walls, uncovering a window into the east parlor. "It's a one-way mirror. We can see them, but they can't see us." Sofia flipped a speaker switch next to the window. "Now we can hear them, too." She grinned at Adam and said, "This club is fun. *If* you're one of the special club members who are in the know. And now you are, Adam."

Adam looked at Sofia, not entirely understanding. Then he looked through the one-way mirror into the east parlor. He gasped at what he saw.

Victor and Maddie were locked in a passionate embrace, his mouth covering hers, his large black hands exploring her petite body.

Sofia looked at Adam and saw the excitement in his face. She smiled, shaking her head in disbelief. "You really like this, don't you?" She looked down and saw the tent formed in Adam's pants. "You like watching your wife with another man."

Sofia reached down and unzipped Adam's pants, pulling out his hard dick. He moaned as she wrapped her hand around his shaft.

She glanced back at the window. Victor had pulled Maddie's skirt up around her waist, completely revealing the young blonde's long stocking-clad legs. "Maddie's legs are soooo nice," Sofia cooed admiringly, and Adam nodded in agreement. Adam watched breathlessly as Victor snaked his hand into his wife's panties, the filmy material straining against the black man's large hand.

"Ohhh godddd," Maddie moaned over the speaker as Victor fingered her.

"Get on your knees!" Victor commanded. "Suck my cock!"

Sofia watched Adam as Maddie got on her knees and pulled Victor's cock out of his pants. She smiled when she saw the amazed expression on Adam's face. "My husband's really big, isn't he?" she said, her eyes not leaving Adam's face.

Adam glanced at her, and as he did Sofia squeezed his penis, causing him to look down. Sofia cupped his penis, almost all of it fitting within her small hand. Then Sofia looked back through the window, Adam following her gaze. Even with both her hands, Maddie struggled to hold Victor's long, thick, heavy shaft. The size difference was startling. Adam looked back at Sofia, and he found her looking at him, an amused expression on her face. Adam's cheeks flushed red in embarrassment.

They heard a gagging sound over the speaker and turned back to the window. They saw Maddie with her mouth wide, trying to swallow Victor's bulbous cockhead. She managed to swallow his cockhead and part of his shaft, but most of his shaft remained outside her mouth. He was too thick to swallow down her throat, and she gagged whenever Victor tried to stuff more in. Saliva flowed down her chin and covered her hands, the diamond of her engagement ring glistening from the slick moisture.

Adam panted excitedly, his eyes glued on his wife as she sucked Victor. Sofia was wet watching Adam watch Maddie and Victor. "You like watching Maddie suck Victor, don't you?" she said breathlessly.

"God yeah," Adam grunted.

Victor pulled Maddie to her feet. His big black cock swung heavily back and forth as he moved Maddie across the room until she faced a billiards table. He bent her at the waist so her tits pressed against the table's velvet surface, and then pulled her skirt up past her ass. With his foot, he pushed Maddie's legs apart, the sound of her high heels scraping across the waxed hardwood floors being audible over the speaker.

Maddie gripped the sides of the table, bracing herself, as she felt Victor pull her panties to the side and position his cockhead at the lips of her pussy. "Ughhhh godddd!" she gasped as Victor penetrated her.

"Oh god, oh god!" Maddie wailed as Victor impaled her on more of his thick shaft.

Victor wrapped his black fingers in Maddie's blonde hair and pulled her head back so they were cheek to cheek. "You love my cock, don't you bitch!" Victor hissed. "You want more of my big black cock, don't you?"

"Oh god, yes!" Maddie begged. She reached back and grabbed Victor's pants, pulling him towards her. "Give it *all* to me!"

Adam and Sofia watched as, inch-by-inch, Victor's cock disappeared into Maddic's pussy. Finally, he was completely inside, and then he began to pound her. Maddie gripped the sides of the table as Victor savagely fucked her, her pretty face pressed against the velvet surface of the pool table.

Adam focused on his wife's slim legs. Bent at the waist, her garter snaps dug into her tight ass. With each of Victor's thrusts, she was lifted out of her heels. Then, after a particularly savage thrust, Maddie's high heels fell off her feet, and without interrupting their fucking rhythm, Victor kicked the shoes away. Maddie had to stand on her tippy-toes as Victor continued his onslaught, and Adam marveled at the sexiness of his wife's long shapely legs as her thigh and calf muscles tensed with each of Victor's thrusts into her pussy.

"Oh god, I'm gonna cum!" Maddie cried.

"Not yet!" Victor growled. "I want you to look at me when I make you cum!"

Victor pulled out and twisted Maddie around, so she faced him, pulling her legs around his waist. They both moaned as he shoved the full length of his cock back into her pussy with a single lunge.

They started fucking again, but while just as desperate, their movements weren't as frantic. Victor gently cradled Maddie's head in his hands, his lips covering hers, his tongue playing with hers. Maddie's legs were tightly wrapped around Victor's waist, and her hands caressed Victor's shoulders and neck.

"They're making love now," Sophie observed as she, like Adam, watched Victor with Maddie.

Sophie's words made Adam's heart ache, even as he moaned and felt frenzy with lust.

In just a few more moments, both Victor and Maddie tensed, and then they came together, their backs arching, each panting and moaning into the other's mouth. After cumming they didn't pull apart, but instead remained wrapped in each other's arms. Finally, Victor pulled out, and from his vantage point Adam could see Victor's thick milky seed gush out of his wife's pussy.

"Oh my god," Maddie giggled as she stood, feeling Victor's sperm run down her leg. Within moments her stocking tops were soaked. "I can't go out there," she said, concern in her voice. She tugged her skirt down, but her stockings were laddered at the knees from kneeling on the floor, and Victor's sperm was running farther down her legs.

Victor chuckled. "Don't worry. Come on, we'll go out the back way."

"Wait, I have to find Adam."

Victor waved his hand dismissively. "Don't worry about him. I'm sure he's having fun with Sofia."

Victor saw the look of disbelief in Maddie's face and laughed. "You don't think this is the only empty room, do you? I'm sure your husband has been completely occupied with Sofia. I didn't see him in the crowd, did you?"

Maddie looked troubled. "No, but ... I should call him, tell him where we're going."

Victor looked annoyed. "Whatever. Tell him we're going to the Zebra Club. But do me a favor. Take off your wedding and engagement rings."

"What?"

"It aggravates me, to see you wearing those rings when you're with me. When you're with me, you're with me. You're not with him."

"But ... he's my husband."

Victor scoffed impatiently. "Where was he when Suzanne lashed out at you? Did he come to your side, defend you? No. I did. Where is he now? He's not with you, he's with Sofia. Listen, it's all about respect. After what I've done for you—after the pleasure I've given you – I'm asking for some respect. That's all."

Maddie looked uncertain. Then, hesitantly, she pulled off her wedding and engagement rings, and put them into her purse.

Victor smiled. "Good," he said approvingly. He took her hand – her ringless left hand – and led her from the room.

IN VICTOR'S CAR, MADDIE called Adam. She said, "Hi honey. Victor is taking me to the Zebra Club. Do you want to go?"

"Sure," Adam said into his cell phone. "Sofia and I will meet you by the valet."

"Oh," Maddie said, sounding guilty. "We've already left. Why don't you meet us there? Sofia knows where it is."

Adam hung up, annoyed they hadn't waited so they could all go together. Forcing a smile onto his face, he offered his arm to Sofia. "They've already left, for the Zebra Club. Shall we go and join them?"

Sofia easily saw through Adam's forced smile. She could tell he was annoyed and hurt. Amused, she shook her head. "I think I'll stay here. Go ahead without me." She smiled knowingly. "I'm sure you'll have fun." Then Sofia described how to get to the Zebra Club.

Adam got into his car and started driving across town. He was actually relieved Sofia wasn't going. He still felt embarrassed, remembering how she had teased him about how small he was compared to Victor. She hadn't said anything directly, but she had teased him nonetheless, having cupped his entire erect penis in one of her hands while they watched Maddie struggle to hold Victor's long heavy rod while using both her hands.

But that wasn't the only reason for his embarrassment. Sofia had seen him get so excited watching his wife with another man. She had seen a part of him he wasn't yet ready to admit to himself, much less reveal to another person. Even worse, he had cum in Sofia's hand as Maddie begged Victor to fuck her even deeper with his long thick cock. The memory caused his penis to stiffen, but also shamed him. He didn't understand these desires. But at that moment, understanding wasn't important to him. He just wanted to get to the Zebra Club so he could continue to watch Maddie with Victor.

MADDIE SHIFTED UNCOMFORTABLY in her heels. Even after freshening up in the bathroom, Victor's cum still leaked from her pussy. Her stocking tops were soaked, and the moisture was edging down her thighs towards her knees. She wanted to take off the stockings, but Victor insisted she leave them on. She worried about Adam's reaction when he discovered she had let Victor have her in the club.

But the soiled stockings were also a thrilling reminder of her recent sex with Victor. The memory made her tingle. God, he was so good! He seemed to know all her erogenous zones. He knew where to touch her, and when, and how hard or soft, and how fast or slow. His body was so nice. Not just his penis, which was amazing, but he was so big and strong, so hard and muscular.

Victor put his arm around her, and the tingling increased. She felt weak-kneed around the black man, and her damp thighs made her feel so naughty. She wanted him again. She craved his body and his touch.

Then she remembered Adam, and she felt guilty. She was happily married. She shouldn't so brazenly desire another man, even if she did have her husband's permission. Her thumb touched her ring finger – her *ringless* ring finger – and her feelings of guilt increased.

She nervously glanced around the room. Had Adam arrived? Had he seen she wasn't wearing her wedding and engagement rings? She chided herself. Victor was supposed to be just a fuck partner, someone to play with while Adam played with Sofia. A friend with benefits, that's all. It wasn't right to have such strong feelings and desires for him. She shouldn't have taken off her rings.

Maddie saw Adam enter the club and waved. "Adam's here," she said to Victor.

"Where's Sofia?" Victor asked as Adam approached alone.

"She wanted to stay at the club, so she didn't come."

Victor broke into a big smile. "Maybe not yet, but she'll be *cumming* soon." He laughed at his joke. "I told you she's a fickle bitch. She's had her eye on the new bartender the club just hired. He's probably banging her in the storeroom at this very moment."

Maddie felt a mix of emotions. A part of her was relieved. She didn't want her husband with the beautiful Sofia, so was glad she moved on to a new partner. Another part of her was anxious. How would this work now? With Sofia moving on to someone else, would Victor move on too? Maddie found (with no small amount of guilt) that she didn't like that idea. The cravings of her body couldn't be turned off like a light switch. She still desired Victor.

Victor seemed to read her mind. "Now we can have even more fun," he said with a lecherous smile on his face.

"What do you mean?" Maddie asked, feeling both excited and a little scared. Her lovely blue eyes grew wide as Victor told her what he had in mind.

"Now you've got both me and Adam, all to yourself," he said, looking first at Maddie, then at Adam. "Two is fun. Three is better. Let's go to my house and I'll show you both how much fun we can have."

Victor convinced the couple to stay for a couple drinks (to help reduce anxieties as this would be the first time the three would be together without Sofia), and then they decided to take a taxi to avoid DUIs. Maddie was sandwiched between Victor and Adam in the back seat. Maddie fidgeted nervously. While her body longed for another go with Victor, she knew she would be self-conscious with Adam there. Also, she didn't know how to handle the wedding ring issue. She covered her left hand with her right, not wanting Adam to see she was ringless.

Victor noticed Maddie's nervousness, and her attempts to hide her left hand. He inwardly chuckled, having dealt with this situation before.

"Adam, I asked Maddie to take off her wedding rings when she's with me. You don't mind, right?" Victor said it as a question, but it came out sounding like a command.

Adam was thrown off-guard, surprised at Victor's directness. He looked at Maddie's ring finger but she was covering it with her right hand. "That's okay, I guess," he blurted out without thinking.

Maddie looked surprised, and then troubled. Before she could say anything, she felt Victor place an arm around her, and then he kissed her cheek. "See, honey, I knew Adam wouldn't mind. He understands, when you're with me, you're with me. Right Adam?"

"Yeah, sure," Adam said, trying to hide his annoyance. He didn't like Victor calling Maddie "honey," but he thought he'd look foolish protesting, given everything else.

"Adam, get us some drinks, okay?" Victor said as soon as they arrived at his house. Again, Victor said it as a request, but it came out as a command. Victor winked at Adam. "Your pretty wife and I will meet you in the living room."

Adam went to the wet bar and pulled out glasses and a bottle of Grey Goose. But the bar's icemaker was off. It took a while to go to the kitchen to get ice as it was on the other side of the palatial house. By the time Adam finally arrived in the living room with a tray of martinis, at least 15 minutes had passed.

Victor and Maddie were on the sofa, making out. As they French kissed, Victor's hand fondled her breasts. She was braless under her dress (her bra probably still in the club's bathroom after Sofia took it off her), and Victor rubbed her erect nipples as they protruded through the dress's stretchy material.

Adam was annoyed. He had assumed they would wait for him. He cleared his throat to announce his arrival, and the couple pulled apart.

Maddie looked guilty that they had started without him. She hadn't wanted to, but as soon as they sat down, Victor had pulled her to him. She was finding she couldn't resist him, and that made her feel even more guilty.

Victor chuckled as he sensed Maddie's discomfort. He motioned at Adam's crotch. A tent was formed in his pants. "See, honey, I told you Adam wouldn't mind if we started without him. He likes watching you with other men – especially black men—don't you Adam?"

Adam flushed red at having been outed, and he wasn't able to meet his wife's eyes when she looked questioning at him.

Victor chuckled again and grabbed a martini, draining it in a single gulp. "Weed?" Victor asked, pulling out a pipe and filling it with weed. He lit it and took a long drag, then he offered it to Maddie.

Adam almost protested. It didn't take much to get his petite wife stoned, and the drug always increased her horniness. He didn't like the way the evening was going. Maddie wasn't wearing her wedding ring. Worse, Victor had humiliated him in front of his wife. But Adam didn't want to respond to Victor's statement that he liked watching Maddie with other men and weed seemed to be a good way to change the subject. When Maddie looked at him, he nodded his head yes.

Victor brought the pipe up to Maddie's lips. She took a tentative short puff. When Victor didn't remove the pipe, she took a longer drag. She closed her eyes as she felt the drug quickly move through her system, her body tingling, her skin becoming extra sensitive. The pipe was removed, but then she felt something else against her lips. It was the rim of a martini glass. She opened her lips and let Victor slowly pour the vodka down her throat. Then Victor brought the pipe to her lips again, and she took another long drag.

Victor motioned to the sofa, and Adam sat next to him. Then he looked back at Maddie. "Stand up," Victor commanded. "Take off your dress."

Maddie's head was spinning. The marijuana and vodka were clouding her thoughts. Yet, her body still burned with sexual desire, the lustful longings intensified by the weed working through her body. She knew it was wrong to undress for another man, especially with Adam being so near. But that voice inside her was muted by the vodka and pot. Her body desired sex, she needed fucked.

In her dazed state, she rationalized that she couldn't get fucked until she took off her clothes. So she stood, unsteady in her high heels. She reached behind her with both hands. In her dazed state, it took longer than usual, but finally she managed to pull down the zipper. Then she wiggled out of the tight Lycra dress. She stood in just her panties, garter belt, stockings and heels.

Adam's eyes were drawn to the crusty off-white film that had dried on his wife's panties and stocking tops. He immediately recognized it; Victor's dried sperm. His cock grew uncomfortably hard in his pants. He saw how Victor's influence over his wife was growing. He suspected this night was going to turn out bad, and he knew he should grab Maddie and get the hell away. But he couldn't take his eyes off the dried cum on his wife's stocking tops. Despite all his misgivings, he knew he needed to watch Victor fuck Maddie again.

Maddie saw where Adam was looking. She looked down and saw the dried cum on her nylons. Even through the alcohol and weed haze, she grew alarmed. She blushed and moved to take off the stockings. "I told you to leave them on," Victor said, his voice low but firm and commanding.

Maddie hesitated, her fingers lingering on the snaps of her garter belt. She didn't know what to do. She desperately wanted to take off the stockings, to remove from her husband's eyes the evidence of her earlier sex with Victor.

Victor smiled. He was enjoying himself immensely. It was so easy to manipulate white married couples like Adam and Maddie. So easy, and so much fun. He had pegged Adam as a cuckold early on. And Victor loved fucking the white wives of white, cuckold husbands. Especially a wife as attractive as Maddie.

He glanced at Adam. "You want your wife to leave the stockings on, don't you?"

Adam still hadn't been able to take his eyes off his wife's cum-soiled stockings. "Yes," he said in a hoarse whisper, his throat dry. "I want her to leave them on."

Victor's smile broadened. He looked into Maddie's eyes. "See honey, nothing to worry about. Now come here. Get on your knees."

Maddie hesitated again. Through the fog of the pot and vodka, it felt wrong. She wasn't wearing her wedding ring. She had another man's sperm dried on her panties and stockings. This was all wrong.

Victor sensed Maddie's continued reluctance. He turned to Adam. "Don't you agree, Adam? Maddie should kneel down in front of us?"

Adam was panting. Maddie looked so good standing in nylons and heels. The cum stains on her stocking tops heightened his excitement. These desires bothered him, but now was not the time to think about it. "Yeah, Maddie," he said breathlessly. "Victor's right. Get down on your knees, right here in front of us."

Victor smiled triumphantly. "See, honey?" he said soothingly. "Adam agrees with me." He gestured at Adam's crotch, where his erection formed a tent in his pants. "It excites him."

Looking confused, Maddie got onto her knees.

"That's a good girl," Victor said approvingly. "Adam, slide closer to me. That's right. Now Maddie, pull down Adam's pants, and remind him how good your mouth feels."

Maddie pulled down Adam's trousers, and then his underwear. His penis stood straight in the air. She couldn't remember the last time he had been so hard. She wrapped her fingers around his shaft. Adam moaned from his wife's light touch.

"Take him into your mouth," she heard Victor say. "Suck him."

Maddie lowered her head and took Adam's cockhead into her mouth. She pumped his shaft as she sucked him, pleased to hear her husband's moans.

"Finish undressing him," Victor said. "Come on, make him feel comfortable."

Maddie pulled off her husband's pants, socks and shoes. Adam unbuttoned his shirt and tossed it onto the floor.

Maddie lowered her head over her husband's crotch, swallowing his cock again into her mouth. With her nose buried in his pubic hair, she licked Adam's shaft. Adam writhed and moaned as his wife sucked him, loving the sight of his wife's young pretty face buried in his crotch as much as the sensations of his penis in her warm soft mouth.

Victor tapped Adam on his shoulder. "Adam – what do you say – my turn?"

In his lust, Adam couldn't think of anything he wanted to see more than Maddie going down on Victor's big black cock. He wanted to see the black man fucking his wife's pretty, innocent face. He wanted to see Maddie's silky blonde hair swaying back and forth over Victor's jet black thighs as she bobbed her head on his black cock.

"Yeah," Adam panted. He pulled Maddie's mouth off his cock. She looked at him. "It's Victor's turn."

Maddie hesitated. She felt uncomfortable going down on Victor with Adam sitting right next to him. But she saw the look in Adam's eyes, a mixture of lust and encouragement. He wanted her to go down on Victor. And she couldn't deny her own body's desires. She wanted Victor again.

Maddie reached for Victor's waist and unbuckled his belt. She unzipped his pants. Victor lifted his ass as Maddie pulled down his pants. He was hard, his cock forming a huge mound in his briefs.

Maddie's eyes grew wide. She still wasn't used to his size. Then she reached up and pulled down his briefs. Victor's cock popped out.

"God, you're so big," she admired. Victor was only half hard, his cock like a long thick black python.

"Stroke me," Victor commanded. Maddie reached for him. She held him with both hands, one hand on top of the other. Still her hands couldn't completely cover his long shaft. As she stroked him, he got harder, and even bigger. He became so thick her thumbs couldn't touch her index fingers.

"Suck me," Victor ordered, and Maddie lowered her head over his crotch. Still holding his shaft with both hands, she opened her mouth wide and struggled to swallow his big cockhead.

Adam was mesmerized by the sight of his wife with Victor. He couldn't believe the size of Victor's cock. He had seen it before, but not this close, not sitting right next to him. His gaze shifted uncomfortably between Victor's cock, and his own. The difference was startling. Victor's penis towered above Adam's. The comparison made Adam feel insecure and inadequate.

But for whatever perverted masochistic reason, it also aroused him. He grew harder, and his excitement grew so much he almost started to shake. He wrapped his hand around his cock and began to slowly stroke himself.

Victor noticed Adam's arousal. He knew lots of white cuckold husbands like Adam. It didn't surprise him that Adam got turned on seeing his wife with another man, especially a well-hung black man. "You enjoy watching this, don't you?" he asked derisively.

Adam didn't answer, although the mockery in Victor's voice made him redden with shame. Still, he didn't stop stroking himself. Maddie heard what Victor said and, with Victor's cockhead still in her mouth, she looked sideways at her husband. She saw him playing with himself, red-faced and panting, his eyes locked on Victor's cock in her mouth.

She noticed how easily her husband held his cock with just one hand, his curled fingers forming a cylinder that engulfed his entire erect penis, except for the top of his cockhead. She couldn't help comparing her husband's penis to what she was holding in her hands, what she had in her mouth. She remembered the football players from her teens, and how they looked so nice in their tight pants, their large penises outlined in the stretchy material. Adam's small size had never bothered her before, but she wondered if that was still true.

To her relief, Maddie didn't dwell on these thoughts. She couldn't. As Victor tried to force more of his cock down her throat, it was all she could do to keep from gagging.

Victor pulled off his shirt, then lifted Maddie off the floor. At the same time, he kicked off his pants, briefs and socks. Both Victor and Adam were completely naked now, sitting side-by-side on the sofa, while Maddie remained in just her nylons, garter belt, panties and high heels.

Victor's powerful arms and core held Maddie suspended above him, her stocking-clad legs straddling his crotch. "Are you ready for it, honey?" Victor said as he slowly lowered Maddie onto his cock. Adam's eyes were drawn to Victor's crotch. He excitedly watched as the black man's huge cock inched toward his wife's pussy.

"Gaaawwwd," Maddie whimpered as Victor penetrated her with his swollen cockhead. Maddie's eyes were closed, and her teeth clenched, as if steeling herself for further penetration by Victor's thick cock.

Victor held Maddie's hips and slowly pushed in and out, each time edging more of his cock inside the young blonde wife. Adam slowly stroked himself, matching the pace of Victor as he pumped in and out of his wife.

Beads of sweat formed on Maddie's forehead, and she tightly clutched Victor's bulging biceps as if to balance herself. Victor's pace quickened and soon almost all his cock was buried inside Maddie's pussy.

Adam couldn't believe Maddie had taken all of Victor inside her. How could it all fit? Adam looked down again and saw Maddie's pussy stretched tight around Victor's thick rod, her pussy molded around the large veins running up his shaft. Adam's erect penis excitedly twitched in his hand. Adam loosened his grip, not wanting to cum too fast.

"Let me down," Maddie said, moving Victor's hands off her hips. Up to that point, Victor's strong arms had supported most of her weight. Any good sense Maddie had left was buried in her frenzied lust for Victor's muscular body and huge cock. She wanted him, needed him. Maddie got on her knees that straddled Victor's muscular thighs, and then began to move slowly up and down on Victor's long thick shaft. With his hands free, Victor cupped and fondled Maddie's tits, rubbing her erect nipples between the thumbs of his jet black hands.

Maddie moaned as Victor fondled her tits. She increased her pace. Adam looked at his wife. She seemed to be in another world, ecstasy painted on her pretty face. Adam hadn't ever seen Maddie look that way before. It was like she was suspended in a continuous orgasm. Adam noticed that, as Maddie rode Victor, she ran her hands over Victor's muscular chest and arms, her manicured nails scratching along his hard pectorals and biceps. Not able to resist, Adam tightened his grip around his shaft and stroked himself faster.

Suddenly, Maddie threw her head back. "Ahhh ahhhh ahhhhhhhh," she moaned as her body tensed. "I'm cuuummming!" Maddie threw her arms around Victor's muscular neck as she rapidly grinded her pelvis against his. Victor placed his hand behind Maddie's head and pulled her lips to his, kissing her. Maddie passionately kissed him back, moaning into his mouth as her orgasm peaked.

Seeing his wife cum on another man's cock, seeing her locked in an embrace with her black lover as her orgasm rippled through her body, it was too much for Adam to take. Grasping his cock even tighter, he pumped twice more. He moaned as he came, his sperm spitting from his cockhead and over his hand.

Maddie panted heavily as she remained locked in Victor's arms. Her head lay against Victor's muscular chest as she tried to catch her breath. She heard Victor chuckle. "Enjoy yourself?" he asked in a contemptuous tone.

Maddie pulled back from Victor and followed his eyes. He was looking at Adam. Adam was breathing heavy too, his hand still wrapped around his penis and covered with sperm. Adam suddenly felt self-conscious and reached for a towel. He released his cock and wiped his hand.

Victor looked down at Adam's crotch and chuckled derisively. Adam's penis was soft now. It had shrunk so much it was almost hidden among the tangle of his public hairs.

"Come on honey, I'm not done with you yet," Victor said to Maddie. He lifted her off his cock and sat her beside him. "Let me feel that hot mouth of yours again," he said as he grabbed the back of her head and pulled her to his crotch.

Maddie lowered her head. Her orgasm had been fantastic, but she wasn't yet satiated, especially with Victor's big cock in her face.

Victor had not cum yet and was still rock hard. With Adam sitting on the other side of Victor, she could see her husband as she licked Victor's shaft.

Adam's cock stirred to life as he watched. As Maddie licked Victor's hard shaft, her eyes darted to her husband's crotch. Adam almost shuddered as he saw his wife's eyes on his penis as she went down on Victor's huge cock. Adam's penis twitched with excitement and got hard again, and he wrapped his hand around his shaft and began stroking himself just like moments before.

Victor pulled Maddie's head off his cock and laid her down on the sofa facing away from Adam, with her high heeled feet touching his naked thigh. He got between her legs and pushed his cock inside her. It was a lot easier for Victor to penetrate her this time as she was loose and soaking wet.

Maddie moaned as Victor rammed his cock into her. "Harder, harder!" she frantically urged. Within moments, Maddie arched her back as Victor's cock sent her over the edge again. "God god gawwwwd!" she cried as waves of orgasmic pleasure ripped through her body.

As she came, she flexed her shapely legs, the stilettos of her high heels digging into Adam's thigh. Adam grimaced from the pain, but he didn't pull his thigh away. Instead, he ran his hand over his wife's shapely calf as he continued to play with himself.

"I'm close, honey!" Victor moaned. "Where do you want it? In your mouth? On your tits?"

"Inside me!" Maddie answered immediately. "Cum inside me!"

"Did you go on the pill?" Victor asked.

"No," Maddie said. "But it doesn't matter. You've already cum so much inside me."

Victor looked over his shoulder at Adam, a mocking, triumphant grin on his handsome black face.

Victor dug his toes into the sofa and, with that extra leverage, pounded Maddie even harder. Adam couldn't help admire Victor's powerful ass and thigh muscles as he relentlessly pounded his wife's pussy. So close to Maddie as another man fucked her, and still caressing her stockinged legs, Adam felt dizzy with lust. Without thinking, he took off Maddie's shoe and pressed his hard penis against the sole of her foot. It felt so good, the warmth of her foot, the silky nylon against his cock.

Victor climaxed, his body jerking violently as he shot jet after jet of his sperm into Maddie's unprotective, fertile womb. Feeling the power of Victor's ejaculation into his wife, Adam came too, shooting his jism into the sole of his wife's foot. Victor buried his thick black cock deep inside Maddie, trapping his black seed inside the fertile womb of Adam's lily white wife. Adam panted breathlessly as he rubbed his cum along his wife's foot with his softening penis, enjoying the feel of his cock against the nylon seam running across Maddie's pretty painted toes.

Maddie felt the wetness on her foot and looked past Victor's broad shoulders. She realized what her husband had done. "Oh Adam ...." she lamented with a sigh, instinctively kicking her husband away.

Victor glanced back at Adam. He laughed. "Adam, didn't your mama teach you about the birds and the bees?"

"That—" Victor pointed at Adam's penis—"goes here"—he pointed at Maddie's pussy. "Not her foot."

Then he looked at Maddie. He had a big grin on his face. He joked, "Or maybe he has really bad aim." Maddie turned her head away from her husband, hiding her grin and doing her best not to laugh at him.

Still looking at Maddie, Victor said, "Or maybe Adam wants only black seed inside you, honey. Not his whitey spunk. A lot of cuckold husbands are into that. They want their white wives bred by black men. Maybe that's why Adam shot off on your foot instead of taking his turn in your pussy."

Maddie's eyes got big at what Victor said. She looked at her husband. Her silent question was, *"Is Victor right?"*

Adam looked down at his feet, feeling ashamed and completely emasculated.

***

EPILOGUE

Suzanne scowled at her husband Mark. There he was again, on the other side of the club, flirting with all the young, pretty girls. Suzanne hated those girls. They were all the same—tight young bodies with perky boobs and long shapely legs. She hated those girls.

Or maybe it was Mark she hated. Didn't he realize it was easy to have a tight body when you're young? Wait until those bitches go through childbirth a couple of times, and then see what they look like.

Suzanne knew Mark's efforts with those girls were useless. The country club wasn't fun for them anymore. No one wanted to swing with them.

She sighed inwardly, knowing it was *her* fault. Mark was still handsome enough, but she was no longer pretty and sexy like before. She *had* gone through childbirth, not two but three times, and they took their toll on her body. Men didn't desire her anymore.

It hadn't always been that way. It wasn't too long ago that she had a body that men lusted after. Big firm tits, a flat stomach, and shapely legs. Even now, her face was still cute.

But her body wasn't what it used to be, not after having three kids. Her tits were still big, but they sagged after breastfeeding and gravity. She had gained weight around her stomach. She wore long dresses to hide the cellulose and varicose veins that came with the weight gain.

She saw Victor across the room, and a familiar longing washed over her. Just being in the same room with him got her wet. He looked better than ever, and the memory of what he sported inside his pants made her tingle all over.

But it had been a long time since she had been able to enjoy Victor's body, and his manhood. She and Mark used to swing with Victor and Sofia often, and their relationship lasted a long time, long enough for her to have 2 of Victor's babies (the third was Mark's). It was hard having 2 half-black babies. The kids were almost ebony like their father, so it was clear Mark wasn't the father. They were outcasts in their mostly white suburban neighborhood.

Pregnancies are hard on a woman's body, and Suzanne had always struggled with her weight. As her body lost its firmness and she grew plump, Victor lost interest in her.

Suzanne suspected that was why Sofia never had children. Victor insisted his women remain firm and shapely, so Sofia didn't want to risk losing her swimsuit model body.

Suzanne saw Maddie across the room, and a scowl crossed her face. She hated that blonde bitch the most. It wasn't just because she was Victor's slut-of-the-moment. She hated Maddie's beauty.

Maddie was the prettiest girl in the room, by far. Suzanne saw other girls in the room scowling at Maddie as their husbands leered at the beautiful blonde. The dress she wore looked like it was air brushed on her, with a plunging neckline and an extremely short hem. The stiletto heels made her long legs look even longer.

Maddie was even prettier and sexier than Sofia, but the amazing thing was, Sofia didn't seem to mind. Suzanne wondered if Maddie had let Sofia inside her panties yet. Maybe that's why Sofia liked Maddie so much. Suzanne licked her lips as she remembered the things Sofia had done to her, way back when.

Adam stood next to Maddie. Suzanne followed his eyes. Adam was scanning the room, but not looking at girls. No, he was looking at other men. Men who were looking at Maddie.

Adam was practically panting, seeing all the interest other men had for his wife. Suzanne shook her head. It looked like Adam liked swinging so he could watch his pretty wife get fucked by other men. What a cuckold.

She scowled as she saw her husband Mark try to flirt with Maddie. She knew Mark would love to get inside Maddie's panties. Her nostrils flared with anger.

"Maybe it wouldn't be so bad," Suzanne thought to herself. They could have a threesome with Maddie. Cucky Adam could sit in the corner as they took advantage of his wife's body. She'd sit on Maddie's face and make her eat her out, and then as she came, she'd piss on the bitch's pretty face and make her swallow her pee. Suzanne smiled at the thought.

Then maybe Suzanne would fuck Maddie with the strap-on she had. The plastic penis was even bigger than Victor's real thing. Loosen up the blonde slut's pussy so her cuckold husband Adam couldn't feel a thing. Of course, maybe Victor had already ruined sweet Maddie's pussy so Adam couldn't feel anything.

Suzanne looked at Maddie again, studying her. Her dress was so tight it showed every curve. She could make out Maddie's nipples, the bumps of her garter belt ... *god*, she could even see the bitch's camel toe. What a slut! It was obscene to wear such a dress. Even in her prime, Suzanne never wore anything so revealing.

Then Suzanne noticed something else. Was that a slight bump in Maddie's belly? Was she pregnant? If she were, there was no doubt in Suzanne's mind the baby was Victor's. He was the most fertile man on the planet.

Victor liked to say he was fixed. But that was a lie he told husbands so they would let him go bareback with their wives. Victor liked fucking his fertile seed into young white wives. He liked watching them get big with his babies. He liked to fuck them with their big pregnant bellies as their husbands watched helplessly. That turned him on more than anything. He loved permanently changing the lives of married white couples.

Suzanne looked at pretty Maddie with her slim, tight body. A big grin crossed her face as she imagined what Maddie would look like in a few years after having Victor's babies. She won't be as pretty or firm anymore, that's for sure.

Then she looked at Adam. She imagined how sad he would be when men no longer desired his wife. The way men no longer desired her.

These thoughts made Suzanne happy. Maddie would lose her pretty face and sexy body. Men wouldn't desire her anymore. And Adam would lose too, *because* men wouldn't desire her anymore.

Suzanne grinned spitefully. "Maybe the club *is* still fun," she thought delightedly. She looked forward to future club parties to watch as slutty Maddie lost her pretty face and sexy body.

PRINCE CHARMING

ORIGINALLY PUBLISHED as "My Husband, My Life"

MY NAME'S JANIE. I'M 29 now, and I've been married 14 years. My husband Leo's 35. I'm 5'2" and petite.

People tell me I'm pretty. I guess I am. I've always been insecure about my looks.

Part of the reason is my parents were never very supportive. And in school I was always on the fringe of popularity.

I have small breasts, and that didn't help, either with my self-esteem or my popularity. All the popular girls developed big breasts. Or least average size. Mine never got bigger than tiny. It's no fun being called "flat chested" by the mean girls at school.

My family was middle class, but we lived in an affluent suburb. Most of the rich, popular girls thought of me as an after-thought, second class, not worth their time. Middle school and high school were painful for me.

The best day of my life was when I made the cheer team. Suddenly, as a cheerleader, I was popular. I got invited to parties. Popular boys noticed me and asked me on dates.

I lost my virginity to one of those popular boys at one of those parties. I soon found out what they say is true – boys only want one thing. And when they got it from me, they dumped me. That only made my self-esteem worse.

Still, I kept hoping the next one would be my Prince Charming. So, I would open my legs for him. Or my mouth. Usually both.

But every time, after a few dates, I'd get dumped. And now it wasn't just my self-esteem taking a beating. It was my reputation. Word got around I was easy. A sure thing after 2 or 3 dates.

My only real friend on the cheer team was Gemma. I kind of looked up to her because she was a senior and I was a junior. She was sweet to me usually, but sometimes we competed for the same boys and then she would be a real bitch.

A few of times I dated boys after she broke up with them, so when she was mad at me she'd call me "Leftovers Janie." Like all the rest, those boys dumped me too after taking me to bed, and I always felt like they compared me to Gemma, who was prettier, taller, curvier and had bigger breasts than me. So, of course they broke up with me. Why would they want me after being with Gemma?

In my high school you had to get at least a C+ in all your classes, or you couldn't play sports. And yes, cheerleading was considered a sport.

My worse class was math. During my junior year I failed the mid-term math exam, and I was about to be kicked off the cheerleading squad. I felt like my life was ruined. I begged the math teacher, Mr. Gomez, to let me re-take the exam, and he reluctantly agreed.

I studied hard, and the next week I re-took the test. I only got a C-. I was devastated, and knew I'd be kicked out of cheerleading. All the self-worth I had was tied to being a cheerleader. I felt like my life was over and started crying.

That was when I felt Mr. Gomez's hand on my arm. His eyes were on my chest.

"I know cheerleading is important to you," he said. "There might be something you can do to raise your grade ... if you can keep a secret."

"What?" I asked, but I already knew.

Mr. Gomez began rubbing my back, over my bra strap. "Can you keep a secret?" he asked.

"Yes ...," I sputtered nervously. I was afraid.

"I hear you're a friendly girl," Mr. Gomez said as his hand moved to my butt. "Will you be my friend?"

I didn't answer at once. I didn't want to do this. But what choice did I have? I couldn't lose being a cheerleader. I couldn't!

"I'll be your friend," I finally said through trembling lips.

Mr. Gomez locked the door to his class. He came back to me. He turned me so I faced his desk. He pushed me so my chest pressed against this desk. Then he pulled up my skirt. And tugged down my panties.

He fucked me. It didn't take long. He came inside me.

He gave me a B- for the class.

———◆———

I WENT TO A LARGE NORTHEAST college. I majored in dance. My dream was to dance on Broadway someday.

I was still chasing the popular boys, and early my freshman year, I started dating a law student. Keith was a real catch. He was tall and handsome, had a great future as a lawyer, and his parents were well-to-do (they lived in a hugely expensive mansion in Greenwich). He was sweet to me. I began thinking I'd finally met my Prince Charming.

My best friend from high school, Gemma, went to the same college. She was a sophomore, and I was a freshman. We hung out a lot at first, but then she ghosted me. I think because she was jealous I was dating Keith, who everyone knew was a real catch.

Keith took me to a concert. Leo – and this is important, Leo is the man I eventually married – Leo went with us.

Keith and Leo were best friends from Keith's hometown. He was nice, but kind of plain and boring. He was super smart though. Leo was a law student too, and Keith said Leo would probably someday be a Supreme Court judge.

The concert was fun. I talked to Leo some. He was sweet. But all I cared about was Keith. He had all my attention.

⁓⬤⁓

WE WERE ALL A LITTLE drunk when we got back to the frat house. Jake, another frat brother, pushed a big red Solo cup of beer into my hand as soon as we walked in. Keith and Leo went to the next room to see who won the football game. That left me standing with Jake, who soon dragged me onto the dance floor.

Another football game must have started because I didn't see Keith the rest of the night. The frat house was really crowded, and the party was a haze of beer, loud music and more beer.

Jake kept feeding me beers and I got drunk. He kept pulling me onto the dance floor, preventing me from looking for Keith.

As we danced, Jake maneuvered me down a dark hallway. "I'm going with Keith," I said, protesting.

"It's okay, we're just hanging out," Jake said.

Jake dragged me into an empty room. I was drunk, so when he kissed me, I didn't immediately stop him. With his tongue down my throat, he started fondling me, one hand groping my breasts and the other working under my skirt.

I should have stopped Jake, but I was too drunk and, I admit, too horny by that point. Jake pulled up my shirt and blouse and fondled my little tits. Then his hands were under my skirt, tugging my tights and panties down.

The room had an old pool table. He pulled me to the edge of the pool table and pushed so my bare tits were against the worn velvet surface.

Jake took out his cock and pushed into me. He wasn't wearing a condom. He fucked me hard and fast for a few minutes, then came inside me.

I was still laying on the pool table, panting, as he pulled out and zipped himself up. It was like Mr. Gomez, all over again.

But it was even worse. Keith found out and immediately dumped me. Word spread. I was only in the first semester of my freshman year, and I got the reputation of being a slut and a cheat.

Then it got even worse. I found out Gemma set me up. She told Jake about my reputation in high school. So, that's why Jake seduced me, even though he knew I was dating Keith. He just wanted an easy lay. And Gemma wanted to break me and Keith up because she was jealous.

I cried and cried. I was a stupid slut and lost my Prince Charming. And now I had a scarlet letter – C for Cheater – plastered across my forehead.

⬤

THE IRONIC THING IS, I became really good friends with Leo. We kept running into each other and discovered we had a lot in common. He didn't seem to care about what happened with Jake and Keith. Looking back, I think my friendship with Leo saved me.

The next semester, we started casually dating. Sex started soon after.

Leo had a huge crush on me. It was the first time in my life I felt I had the power in the relationship. Leo followed me around like a puppy dog, and he loved my body. He truly lusted after me. Leo was the first man I ever met who actually liked little tits over big ones. To him, my body was perfect. He said I was the prettiest girl he'd ever met.

I wasn't sure of my feelings for Leo. He certainly wasn't popular. He was cute but not handsome. He was barely taller than me. His body wasn't the best. He wasn't fat but he wasn't slim either. He wasn't muscular. His penis was average, maybe a little smaller than average.

But I liked Leo. He was comfortable and fun to be with. And he had money. He had a car. His parents were wealthy. We did a lot of things, and he never asked me to pay for anything.

And he adored me. He absolutely adored me.

It was an *amazing* feeling to be adored. For the first time in my life, someone thought I was really something. Someone thought I was really special.

So, I dated Leo. He made me happy.

Most Fridays we went to the student union happy hour. We avoided going to his frat house because I didn't want to see Keith or Jake. On this particular Friday, Leo was getting us beers when Jake showed up and started hitting on me. His hands were all over me, and he tried to kiss me. I slapped his face and stormed away!

Later that night Leo and I were in bed, making love. He seemed more excited than usual.

"I don't understand why you got so upset," he said as he moved in and out of me. "Jake's harmless."

"Harmless? His hands were all over me! He got me to cheat on David!"

"You can't blame guys for hitting on you. You're a tease."

That surprised me. I grabbed Leo's arms, stopping his movement. "What did you just say?"

"Come on, don't play coy. You're always teasing guys with your hot body. There're a lot of guys who want to get into your pants."

I gawked at Leo. I didn't have a hot body. My body was okay but no one – except Leo –ever called me hot.

"They just think I'm easy," I told him with a frown.

"That's hot too," Leo said. I thought he was joking, but he was serious.

I pushed away from him. "You think it's hot people think I'm easy?" I said getting mad.

"All I'm saying is, guys think you're hot," Leo said. "You should hear what they say about you at the frat."

"What do they say?" I demanded.

Leo began fucking me again, moving slow as he whispered hotly into my ear. "Gang bangs. Cocks in your pussy, ass and mouth. Cumming all over your pretty face."

"They say that?" I asked, horrified. "They think I'm a slut!"

"It's really hot Janie," Leo moaned. A moment later he came.

Later, as we lay in the dark, Leo asked, "Have you cheated on me? Like you did to Keith?"

I turned over to face him. "Leo, we haven't agreed to be exclusive," I said gently. "It's not cheating if I date other boys."

Leo frowned but didn't object. That's how he was. He never disagreed or said no to me. He adored me. I could do no wrong.

I *did* date other guys in addition to Leo. I was still chasing after popular boys, searching for my Prince Charming. I liked Leo, he was fun, but I didn't think he was the one.

I avoided dating guys from Leo's frat. I didn't want to be mean. But still, Leo knew about my dating. It was a small campus.

I'd date a boy a few times. Sleep with him. And after 2-3 weeks he'd dump me. It was always the same pattern. I wasn't good enough. I wasn't girlfriend material. I was an easy fuck, and maybe even a good fuck, but that's all I was.

Then I'd go back to Leo. And he would take me back. Always. He never got mad at me. He never made fun or demeaned me. He would adore me again. He never stopped adoring me.

To me, it made Leo seem desperate. I won't say I lost respect for him because he was my friend. But I began taking him for granted. I knew he'd always be there, no matter what I did.

⸻ ◆ ⸻

FOR SPRING BREAK, I went to Miami with Gemma. We'd made up over the Keith / Jake drama. Gemma apologized and said it was all a misunderstanding. She played all innocent, and I forgave her. What else could I do? She was the closest thing to a best friend I had, and I still looked up to her.

Leo hinted that he wanted to go with us, but Gemma's car was full with me and Gemma and 2 other girls. And I didn't want Leo to go. I was hoping to flirt with boys from other schools, and maybe meet someone special. As always, Leo and I were dating, but like I said, we weren't exclusive. He probably suspected I wanted to meet boys in South Beach. But he never got mad at me or tried to make me feel guilty. He just made me promise to call him as soon as I got home.

Soon after hitting the beach in our bikinis, we met a group of junior boys from Florida State. There were the 4 of us girls and 6 boys so we paired up quickly, with the 2 leftover boys quickly moving on to find unattached girls in other Spring Break groups.

My guy's name was Justin. He was cute and tall and had nice shoulders and pecs. Justin was pre-med. I was dreaming that maybe I'd met my Prince Charming.

Honestly, I don't remember the names of the other boys. I'll just call them Huey, Dewey and Louie. Gemma matched up with Huey. I think she was kind of mad Justin picked me. I don't know why. Huey was better looking. Maybe because Huey was a lit major and didn't – on the surface – seem to have the same career prospects as Justin.

As it got dark, we showered and traded our bikinis for skimpy dresses and strappy high heels. We met up with the boys and I was excited when Justin bought all my drinks, covers and dinner. Maybe he did like me! I started dreaming about transferring to Florida State!

After clubbing for a while, they told us about a party they'd gone to yesterday (they got to South Beach a day before us). Free beer and maybe weed and even blow. I'd never had cocaine before but, well, if my new man Justin wanted me to try it, I would.

The party was kind of a chill vibe in an old 3 story house. It was just the 8 of us plus 2 Puerto Rican guys. They never told me their names.

That seemed kind of weird to me, but beer and weed were everywhere, so I wasn't paying too much attention. Soon I was high and tipsy.

Justin was into me. His hands were on me as we danced, and he kissed me whenever he got the chance. Gemma saw this and got jealous. That's when things got bad for me. Really bad.

Gemma told me the cocaine wasn't free. The 2 Puerto Ricans sold it. She said the boys had been so nice to us, we should treat them to the blow.

That was fine, but I didn't have any money. I never had money. Gemma had promised to treat me to this trip as part of her apology for the Keith/Jake drama. So, what did Gemma want me to do?

She said I should blow one of the Puerto Ricans for the blow. She even laughed about it. A blow for blow.

What?! Why didn't spoiled rich kid Gemma use part of her trust fund to pay for the coke? You know why, right? She wanted to ruin my chance with Justin.

Gemma said I could do it upstairs in one of the bedrooms. No one would ever know. Justin would never know.

And I was stupid enough to do it. Why? Because I'm stupid. And I was drunk and high.

And Gemma was my idol. She was my best friend from high school. I always did what she told me to do.

So, while Gemma distracted Justin, I went upstairs with one of the Puerto Ricans. He sat down on the edge of the bed, I got on my knees, and went down on him.

That would have been it, but when he finished spunking down my throat and I staggered back onto my high heeled feet, everyone was there. Including a grinning Gemma. Including Justin.

Then it got worse. After passing around lines of coke, the other Puerto Rican said he wanted his. And I was the obvious target because I'd already done his friend. It wasn't like Gemma or the other 2 girls were going to let a greasy Puerto Rican boy soil their prissy bodies. Especially since I was already pegged as the slut among the 4 girls there.

The Puerto Rican didn't want mouth, he wanted pussy. He pushed me onto the bed. He jerked down my panties, got between my legs and fucked me. He didn't even use a condom.

Then it was a free for all. Huey, Dewey and Louie wanted theirs. No one helped me. Not Gemma or the other 2 girls. In fact, they laughed and egged on the boys to take me in all my holes.

Justin didn't help me. He didn't do anything to me. He just watched. But he didn't do anything to help me.

I became a cum bucket for Huey, Dewey, Louie and the 2 Puerto Ricans. They fucked my mouth. My pussy. They fucked my ass. None of them used condoms.

Eventually, Justin fucked me too. He pulled out and splattered my face with his cum. As he looked at my soiled, cum soaked body, he said with disgust, "Gemma is right. You're a cheap whore."

<hr>

LEO CAME AND GOT ME. I was a basket case. He flew down to South Beach. He checked us into a hotel. He took care of me. He took me to a hospital to get an STD test. Then we flew home. He paid for everything.

I wanted to quit school. I couldn't stop crying. My life was over. My reputation was ruined. Gemma and the 2 other bitches told everyone. How could I ever show my face on campus again?

Leo wouldn't let me quit. He wouldn't allow me to give up on my dream to dance on Broadway someday.

Leo walked me to my classes. He wanted outside and walked me home. He was constantly by my side, defending me, telling people how it was all Gemma's fault, how she set me up.

Leo wasn't popular, but he was respected on campus because he was smart and had never been caught in a lie. Because of Leo, Gemma's reputation was ruined. *She* was the one who quit school, not me. She transferred to a college on the other side of the country.

From that moment on, Leo became more than just my safety net. More than my second choice or rebound boyfriend.

Leo became my man. *He* was my Prince Charming.

Leo still adored me. He desired me, coveted me. He loved me.

And I fell in love with him. I would do *anything* for him.

And in the coming years, I would do *many* things for him.

⎯⎯⎯◉⎯⎯⎯

THE SUMMER AFTER MY freshman year passed slowly. I went home and got a job lifeguarding at a local pool. It was boring, but I got a great tan. Leo graduated from law school and got a job in one of the big New York law firms. I missed him a lot. I missed his company. His companionship. He was my Prince Charming. I really missed him.

And I missed the sex too. Leo wasn't the best lover I'd ever had. But not the worst either.

Our sex was good. Leo didn't fuck me. He made love to me. And while his penis wasn't the biggest – his was probably a little below average in size – he had a wonderful tongue.

⎯⎯⎯◉⎯⎯⎯

FOR ALL HIS PLUSES, Leo was kind of plain vanilla. So, it surprised me when I realized he liked talking about the boys from my past; the sex I had with those boys.

When he first asked me, I thought it was a trap, like he was going to guilt me about being so easy and slutty. But eventually I figured out it excited him to hear about me with other guys. I didn't understand why he was like that – I still don't, not completely – but I answered all his questions because, like I said, he was my Prince Charming and I would do anything for him.

Surprisingly, talking with Leo made me feel less slutty about my past. It was like, my promiscuity back then was a good thing because it got my Prince Charming so hot.

And Leo's unconditional acceptance of what I did – and *enthusiasm*—made me feel better about myself. During our pillow talk, he never failed to tell me how pretty and sexy I was. He told me that's why those boys wanted to get into my pants. He said things like, "You're so smoking hot, of course every man wants to get you into bed," and "You're not easy, you just like sex, and there's nothing wrong with that."

Leo said things like that so many times, I started to believe him. Maybe I *was* pretty. Maybe I *was* sexy. Maybe I *was* desirable.

Leo even said I had his permission to have sex with other guys. He said the only rule was, I had to tell him about it. I thought he was crazy, and joking, but he said it so much – calling it my *hall pass* – that I began thinking he was serious about it.

Talking with Leo helped my self-esteem and I felt better about myself. We got closer. I fell even more in love with him. I became even more convinced he was my Prince Charming.

That's why I was so excited about Leo's visit in late July. I introduced him as my boyfriend – he *was* my boyfriend—and my parents were immediately impressed with him and his bright future as an attorney. Even my younger brother, who I'd never gotten along with, liked Leo.

The weekend went fast as I introduced Leo to my high school friends (Gemma was nowhere to be seen, thank god). While Leo wasn't the most handsome, he was easily the nicest guy I'd ever dated, and all my friends liked him. By the end of the weekend, I was really proud to be his girlfriend. And of course, I'd do anything for him.

Sunday night, Suzanne's parents were having a BBQ pool party. Suzanne was another cheerleader from high school. One time after a night football game, her father – Mr. Owens—groped me. He reached under my cheer skirt and squeezed my behind. And it wasn't a quick squeeze, he rubbed me and even reached between my legs.

Afterwards, I pretended like it didn't happen and we never talked about it. I never mentioned it to Suzanne of course. From that moment on, I kept my distance from him. It weirded me out whenever I saw him.

When I told Leo this story, he went crazy with lust. He told me I should have let Mr. Owens take me to bed. He said it would have been super-hot, to fuck my friend's father who was more than twice my age. Leo was crazy wild about the idea of me getting Mr. Owens to cheat on his wife. Our sex that night was amazing. For over a week, Mr. Owens was the focus of our pillow talk. Leo was so into it and our sex was so passionate, I started thinking that maybe I *should* have gone to bed with Suzanne's father.

After a few hours at the BBQ party, Leo whispered in my ear, "Mr. Owens has been looking at you all night."

I laughed, thinking we were probably going to have extra passionate sex later that night with more sexy pillow talk about Mr. Owens.

Leo sported a wicked smile. He said, "By the way, his name's Bob. Why don't you thank him for hosting such a fun party? Go upstairs and do what you should have done back in high school."

My eyes went wide with shock. "Are you serious?" I said.

Leo glanced around and said, "It's crowded and getting dark. No one will notice you and Bob are gone. And don't you want to get back at Suzanne and her bitchy mom?"

I'd told Leo that Suzanne was part of the *in-crowd*. She was being nice to me now, but back in high school she was really mean. More than once she made fun of my small breasts, calling me flat chested. And her mom was a bitch too. I heard she lobbied against me making the cheer team, telling our coach I wasn't good enough.

The idea of getting back at Suzanne and her mom appealed to me. But by fucking their father/husband? Here, at their house?

It was a crazy idea. And I was with Leo now. My slutty days were over. I wanted to be a good girl.

Then, looking into my eyes, Leo said, "I want you to do it. Don't worry. I won't hold it against you. I'll love you even more."

It was the first time he said the L word. I'd never said it either, even though I knew I loved him. Maybe it was my low self-esteem, but it was really important that he said it first. And he just did.

But I had to be sure. So, I whispered, "You love me? Really?"

"Yes," Leo said without any hesitation. "I really love you."

"I love you too," I replied.

Leo smiled and squeezed my hand. "I want you to do this," he said.

My Prince Charming loved me. And he wanted me to do something.

I nodded to Leo. I squeezed his hand back. Then I moved towards Mr. Owens.

I found him sitting on a chair by the pool. He looked at me as I approached.

"Hi Mr. Owens," I said to him. "Do you remember me? Janie?"

"Of course I know who you are," Mr. Owens said as he took a sip of his beer.

"Can I talk to you a sec?" I asked. "Inside the house?"

"About what?" he asked suspiciously.

"Remember that time you touched me under my skirt?"

Mr. Owens' eyes got big with alarm. "I don't know what you're talking about!" he hissed.

"I'm not mad," I whispered. "I've thought a lot about it. I think we have some unfinished business."

Mr. Owens' eyes got even bigger, but this time with excitement. "Are you serious? What about your boyfriend?"

I remembered how Leo got so excited by the idea of me getting Mr. Owens to cheat on his wife. So, I gave him a mischievous smile and said, "What about Mrs. Owens? I can keep a secret, if you can."

Mr. Owens grinned. He said, "You know where the guest room is? Meet me there in 5 minutes."

Our sex was fast because it had to be fast. I was wearing a short skirt, similar to the cheer skirt I wore in high school. Inside his guest bedroom, Mr. Owens pressed me against the wall, raised my skirt and tugged down my panties, and then fucked me from behind.

Suzanne's father panted like a fat pig as he banged me. I won't lie, I was getting off on it. All the pillow talk about Mr. Owens had sexualized him in my head, so I wanted him to fuck me. He was Suzanne's father, and her bitch mother's husband. The wickedness was deliciously sinful. I was getting back at all of them, not just Suzanne and her mother, but all the in-crowd.

And the best part was, I was doing it for Leo. I had his permission. He wanted me to do this! He loved me!

I sensed Mr. Owens was close. Just then, wicked inspiration flitted through my head. With my face pressed against the wall and Mr. Owens fucking me hard and fast from behind, I whispered to him, "Do you fantasize about Suzanne? I bet you do. I bet you wish it was her instead of me. I bet you wish you were fucking your daughter."

Mr. Owens grunted and came, exploding inside me. Afterwards, with his penis softening and falling out of me, he said between gasps, "Fuck you're a nasty bitch. A nasty, nasty bitch."

Later that night, Leo couldn't get enough of me. We had to be quiet because we were in my parents' house, but still he fucked me over and over.

He loved what I said to Mr. Owens about fantasizing about his daughter. Loved it! To him, it was even better than getting the faithful husband to cheat on his wife. I was learning my straightlaced Leo had a major kinky thing going on.

Leo also got hot that I didn't make Mr. Owens wear a condom or pull out. To be honest, I didn't have a condom with me, and I was on the pill.

Leo didn't care about those details. He said he loved the fact Mr. Owens' spunk was inside me. Proof that I was a bad girl. And he said Mr. Owens didn't know I was on birth control. Maybe that's what he wanted. Maybe that was part of his fantasy. To impregnant his daughter. I wasn't Suzanne, but maybe Mr. Owens was fantasizing I *was* as he fucked his sperm into me.

Leo loved it all! And he loved me! He said it over and over. For the first time in my life, I felt like someone loved me. *Really* loved me.

In the past, I would feel shitty about what I'd done with Mr. Owens. And slutty. I'd feel like a nothing, not worth anything.

But Leo loved how slutty I'd been! Loved it! To him, slutty was good!

Leo's unconditional acceptance of me really boosted my ego. He made me feel good about myself. My self-esteem was at an all-time high.

He reminded me I had a hall pass. I had his permission to have sex with other guys. I just had to tell him about it.

I wasn't sure. Did he want an open relationship? I didn't want that. I didn't like the idea of Leo with other girls. I'd always been a jealous person. And especially with Leo. He was my Prince Charming. His dick belonged to me, and only me. As far as I was concerned, his dick would never be in another girl's hand, mouth, pussy or ass. Only mine.

I didn't get into it with Leo. Not at that moment. Our relationship was still young, and I didn't want him to think I was a crazy, jealous girlfriend. Also, in the past, it was me who didn't want to be exclusive. If I tried to force Leo into that now, he might think less of me. Like, he might think I was desperate. I knew I still had to play hard to get, even though I was madly in love with him. *Especially* since I was madly in love with him.

LEO AND I WERE A COUPLE throughout my sophomore, junior and senior years in college. He lived in New York City, working for that big law firm. We saw each other every weekend, and spent every holiday together. During summers I lived with him and interned at dance studios. My parents loved Leo and supported my relationship with him. He even grew close to my brother, and sometimes we'd go on double dates. I also grew close to Leo's family, getting to know his mother and father really well, and also becoming good friends with his younger brother Drew.

I graduated and immediately moved in with Leo. I auditioned for shows on Broadway, and got a few small parts. The gigs hardly paid anything, but I didn't need to make money because Leo was doing so well in his law firm. Leo encouraged me to keep dancing because he loved it when I came home from a rehearsal all hot and sweaty in my leotard and tights.

Leo bought me a new wardrobe every season. I had four closets in his apartment, and they were all bursting with outrageously expensive designer mini-skirts, short dresses and revealing blouses, as well as dozens of high heels by *Jimmy Choo, Prada, Christian Louboutin* and *Manolo Blahnik*. He also spent thousands on lingerie, throwing out my pantyhose and tights and buying big shopping bags of expensive garter belts, stockings and thigh highs.

We went out almost every night to expensive bars, restaurants and shows. My friends were envious of my lifestyle, and constantly told me how lucky I was to be with him. But it was more than just the expensive clothes and restaurants. Leo was the kindest and most supportive man I'd ever met. We shared every hope, dream and secret, and became very close. We were soulmates. My love for Leo grew and grew.

We played kinky games, ones that got Leo hot. I did whatever he wanted me to do, because I loved him, and wanted to keep him hot for me.

Often, we played a game where we'd go to a bar separately. Leo liked to watch as men hit on me. I liked it too. All the male attention boosted my ego and liked Leo watching me. I liked being the center of his world.

Soon into this game I learned the incredible effect a lacy stocking top has on men. I quickly became an expert at "accidentally" flashing a little stocking top at my suitors. It usually happened at that brief moment of time between crossing my legs and adjusting my skirt. I'd look away at that moment, because I didn't want to catch him staring (as that would give me away), but sometimes via the mirror behind the bar I'd see the men looking, their eyes full of lustful desires. Just thinking about it makes me moist.

I also came to realize that many men have a fetish over feet. Leo always complimented me on my feet, saying they were sexy because they were petite and slim, smooth and unblemished. One time as we were cabbing to a bar to play our game, Leo encouraged me to show off my feet, and suggested a few ways to do it. I thought he was crazy, but when I did it, I couldn't believe the reaction it had on men. As I stood talking to two guys, I lifted my foot from my high heel, not a lot, just an absentminded motion like the waving of your hand as you're talking. The two guys gawked at my stockinged foot, and the men behind them were practically panting and didn't take their eyes off my legs and feet, I guess hoping for a repeat performance.

Our game always resulted in great, passionate sex. Leo still encouraged me to have sex with other men. He was relentless, telling me over and over that's what he wanted. I never did though, other than that one time with Mr. Owens.

I think Leo was growing frustrated. He wanted me to take our game to the next level. He wanted me to go home with one of those men I flirted with in bars. He was getting tired of hearing about my past experiences. He wanted *new* experiences, like what I'd done with Mr. Owens. Although even that was years ago.

I didn't want that. Leo was all I needed. For me, flirting and even a little touching with others were more than enough. I didn't go as far as Leo wanted, but our games *did* add spice to our sex life. Our life was idyllic, we were in love, and I longed for the day Leo would ask me to marry him.

Then everything changed.

I had just turned 24, and we were at a restaurant with Danny, another lawyer where Leo works. Danny reminded me of Jake from college, nice looking but extremely confident to the point of being arrogant, the stereotypical lawyer. Despite being so different and often competing as rivals for the same projects and promotions, Leo and Danny often hung out together.

Our waitress was a tall pretty blonde wearing a crisp white blouse and a black micro-mini skirt. More than once I caught Leo ogling her long legs (she wore black tights and Mary Jane high heels). I grew annoyed, especially when Leo and Danny started to openly flirt with the waitress. She couldn't have been a day over 19. It's funny. I was still a young woman but looking at the waitress and her fresh good looks and bubbly personality, I felt old. I fumed when Leo seemed to linger over the menu as an excuse to continue flirting with the young waitress. I lost it when Leo leaned towards the girl, in the process pressing his arm against the girl's abundant chest.

"Why don't I leave so you can be alone with her!" I said angrily to Leo once she'd left.

Leo didn't say anything, but Danny laughed. "Oh, come on Janie, we're just having some fun. Did you see her chest? How can someone so thin have tits that big? My god, they must be double-Ds!"

I felt hurt inside. Leo knew I was insecure about my small breasts. "Is that what you want, Leo, a pretty blonde with big breasts?" I glared at him to hide the hurt inside. "Well, sorry, I stopped stuffing my bra back in junior high!"

Danny roared at that. Leo sheepishly smiled. They were both drunk, and I'd had enough. I got up and left the bar, intending to catch a cab home.

Just then a figure entered the cab. I hoped it was Leo, coming after me to apologize, but it was Danny. "Come on Janie, you can't leave by yourself, this is New York City, it's not safe."

"Where's Leo?"

"He's giving you some room to cool down." Danny had a big grin on his face. "He said something about you having a nasty temper."

I looked away. I *did* have a nasty temper, mostly when I got jealous (like now), but I didn't appreciate Leo telling people about it. "Whatever," I said dismissively. "He probably just wants to flirt with the waitress some more."

Danny shrugged, the smile still on his face. "What can I say, boys will be boys. Come on, you can crash at my place tonight. I have a spare bedroom."

Danny handed me a big glass of white wine as soon as we entered his apartment. I sat down and took a big gulp of the wine. I wondered what Leo was doing, whether he was at that moment having sex with the 19-year-old waitress. I felt angry and hurt, and it wasn't all about tonight.

By that time, we'd been dating over 5 years; 3+ years in college, and 2 years since. In all that time, Leo's eye had never wandered; I'd always been the center of his attention. But lately he'd been distant, even bored. We hadn't had sex in a while, and I'd seen him looking at other girls. I felt terrible, wondering if Leo was getting ready to break up with me.

"Want some of this?"

I looked up, having forgotten about Danny. He held a joint.

"Sure," I said, holding out my hand. But instead of giving me the joint, he brought it to my lips. "Whatever," I thought still distracted over Leo, accepting the joint between my lips and taking a long drag.

I left lipstick around the joint. Danny didn't seem to care. He took a long puff as he sat down next to me. I took another long sip of wine, then opened my lips again as Danny brought it to my mouth. This went on for about 10 minutes, Danny taking a drag, then me, then a sip of wine, then back to Danny. Soon I felt the warm comfortable haze of the weed flowing through my body. My troubles with Leo hadn't gone away, but they felt like a distant memory.

I leaned back into the couch and closed my eyes. I felt something on my lips, and I thought it was the joint, but realized Danny was kissing me. "Danny, stop," I said pulling away.

"Come on baby," Danny said, pulling me to him. "What's a sexy girl like you doing with a loser like Leo? You're way too hot for him."

"Stop Danny," I repeated as he pressed his lips against mine and shoved his tongue into my mouth. Danny cupped my breasts. "Stop," I said again, pulling away.

Danny's eyes moved to my thighs. In pulling away from him I had inadvertently hiked up my skirt, and my stocking tops were showing. I pulled down my skirt, but it was too late, Danny was frenzied with lust. He batted away my hands and pushed my skirt up around my waist, exposing my lacy panties, garter belt and stockings.

"Fuck you're a sexy girl," he admired as he plunged his tongue into my mouth.

"Danny, I said stop!" I protested again.

Danny finally pulled away. "You're too good for Leo," he said. "He doesn't appreciate you. You know he's having an affair with Lilly?"

"You're lying," I said. Lilly was Leo's new secretary. I got up and pulled down my skirt, unsteady in my heels due to the lingering effects of the marijuana.

"I'm not lying," he insisted. "You saw how Leo acted tonight with that waitress. Face it, he likes young girls. Lilly's 18, just out of high school. You've seen her. She's blonde and pretty, with long legs. She's just like you, except a lot younger."

I felt tears forming in my eyes. Could it be true? But then I knew it *was* true. Leo's wandering eyes had always fallen on young girls. And I knew Leo's type – pretty leggy blondes. Lilly reminded me of me, except she was 18, and I was 24. Tears rolled down my cheeks as I realized my relationship with Leo was ending.

Danny came to me and wiped away my tears with his hand. "Leo's an idiot. You're way hotter than Lilly. Leo's a loser, he doesn't know what he's got."

Danny led me to his bedroom, and I followed in a stupor. I didn't have the will to resist. He undressed me to my lingerie and laid me on the bed. "You're so fucking hot!" he said admiring my body. "You have no idea how long I've wanted you." He took off his shirt, revealing a muscular chest, and then his pants. Despite my despair, I couldn't help noticing the size of his penis. He was huge. Much bigger than Leo.

Seeing my expression, Danny smiled. "I've seen Leo in the gym," he said with contempt. "Tonight, you're going to see what it's like to be with a real man."

Danny's words vibrated through my head. Something inside me snapped, and my jealousy and heartache turned to anger. I knew I was pretty and had a sexy body. Leo had taught me that.

"Fine Leo, you go and chase after all the teenage girls you want," I thought. *"Let me tell you something, they'll get older, and we'll see how good they look then."*

"Come here," I said to Danny, rolling off the bed and onto my knees. Danny smiled, and when he approached, I took his cock in my hands. He was so big I needed both hands to hold him. I took him into my mouth, stroking his shaft as I sucked on his cockhead. He reached down and expertly unsnapped my bra. I detached myself from his cock long enough to let the bra fall from my arms and onto the floor. I saw the lust in his eyes as he lecherously gawked at my small perky breasts. "Fuck you're gorgeous!" he gushed. "You're perfect!"

I beamed inside. I hadn't realized how much I missed the adoration of men, something that had been missing so long from Leo as our relationship grew stale. It'd been years since I'd held a penis other than Leo's, and I planned on enjoying myself.

Danny pulled me up and laid me on the bed. I curled my toes in my heels to keep my Jimmy Choos from falling off, because I could tell Danny was a man who liked to fuck a girl wearing high heels. Danny pulled my panties down my legs and stared at my pussy, which I kept bare except for a tiny landing strip above my clit. "Beautiful!" he said, and he moved between my legs. He lifted my legs to his shoulders, his hands running up and down my nylons. "You have no idea how long I've wanted to do this," he said looking into my eyes.

He reached over to his night table and picked up a condom. I put my hand over his. "That's okay, you don't need to use that. I want to feel you cum inside me."

Danny grinned. "You really want to get back at Leo, huh?"

I raked my manicured nails along Danny's muscular chest. "I just want to feel you inside me. Now fuck me – please. I'm so hot for you." And I realized I was telling the truth. The lack of sex with Leo, Danny's beautiful body, and the weed were making me horny as hell. I wanted to feel Danny's incredible cock inside me, I wanted to cum all over his thick shaft, I wanted to feel him shoot his sperm inside me.

I reached between my legs and took hold of his shaft, guiding him to me. He pushed hard and I grunted from his size as he penetrated me. For years, I'd only had Leo's smallish penis – the only exception was Mr. Owens—and I felt like a virgin again.

I grimaced as his fat cockhead penetrated me. He was big!

"Oh god," I moaned as he inched his long shaft inside me. I was stretched so tight around his thick cock I could actually feel the wide veins running along his shaft. "Faster!" I urged him, running my nails up and down his muscular arms. "Harder, faster!" I begged.

Within moments I felt Danny's body tense, and then he violently lunged into me, once, twice, over and over, his fertile seed splashing against the walls of my fertile womb. I wrapped my arms and legs around him, urging him deeper inside me, bringing his lips down to mine so we could seal our fucking with the intimacy of a kiss.

Two hours later I stepped into our apartment, the one I shared with Leo. I wondered how much longer I would live there. After tonight, I expected Leo would dump me. Trade me in for a younger girl.

I had let Danny fuck me twice more, each time bareback, each time letting him cum inside me. I carried my high heels in my hand. I had worn the heels while Danny fucked me and only taken them off in the cab. My stockings were laddered and semi-detached from my garter belt. I was braless under my untucked blouse, and panty-less under my skirt. My pussy was red and moist from Danny's sperm. My blonde hair was a mess and my makeup long gone. Hickeys were all over my neck, Danny having marked me as his fuck toy for the night. In other words, I was freshly fucked, and I wanted Leo to see me that way.

I walked into our bedroom – Leo's bedroom now – expecting to see him with Lilly or the waitress, or some other "barely legal" blonde. Instead, I found him reading, apparently waiting for me. He looked up and stared at me. He got up and walked to me. He pulled my blonde hair back, inspecting my neck, seeing Danny's hickeys. "You've been with Danny," he said, stating the obvious.

Tears gushed down my cheeks. "And you've been screwing Lilly, you shit!" I sobbed, feeling like my life was over, waiting for him to drop the bomb that we were over.

Unexpectantly, Leo laid me on the bed. As I sobbed, he straddled my hips and slowly unbuttoned my blouse. He stared at my bare breasts, running his fingers lightly over the red splotches that evidenced Danny's rough handling. He pressed down against my nipples, rolling them between his fingers. "They're so swollen," he said. "Danny sucked them hard, didn't he?"

I stopped sobbing as Leo continued his inspection of my body. He pulled down my skirt, then carefully ran his fingers along the runs in my stockings. "He must've fucked you hard to do this to your stockings," he said.

Then Leo moved between my legs. Suddenly feeling ashamed, I covered my well used pussy with my hands, but Leo pushed them away. "Your pussy lips are so swollen," he marveled. He ran a finger along the wetness. "You let him fuck you without a condom. And cum inside you."

Leo pulled out his penis and entered me. "How many times did Danny fuck you?" he asked.

I turned away, but Leo pulled my head back to look at him. "Tell me!" he demanded, looking into my eyes.

"Three times," I finally admitted.

"He make you cum?"

"Yes," I said. Thinking about Lilly and feeling spiteful, I said, "Danny's cock is bigger than yours."

Rather than being upset, Leo moaned, "Oh god, really?"

I felt things shifting between me and Leo. When we first met, I had all the power. Then, after what happened in South Beach with Gemma, the power in our relationship shifted to Leo.

Now, I felt the power shifting back to me. I felt Leo's attention shifting back to me.

I said, "Oh yeah. He made me cum hard. And Danny's body is hot. He's so muscular." I ran my fingertips over Leo's arms and chest, feeling the softness where with Danny it had been hard and defined. "Your body's soft, Leo. Not hard like Danny's."

"Oh god Janie!" Leo moaned.

"I missed it, you know? Being fucked by a hard body. A big cock. And he's so good in bed. He reminded me what great sex is like."

"Oh god, I'm cumming!" Leo screamed.

After he was finished, Leo hugged and snuggled me. The way he hadn't in a long time.

Leo tried to kiss me, but I wouldn't let him. I said, "Tomorrow, you're firing Lilly."

"Okay," Leo agreed immediately.

I said, "If you ever flirt with a girl like you did tonight, I'll leave you and move in with Danny. I should anyways. He fucks me better than you."

"Don't do that," Leo begged, trying to kiss me again. This time I let him.

I was still angry and hurt about tonight, but now I was the center of Leo's world again. He adored me again. I had the power again.

———◉———

LEO DIDN'T FIRE LILLY. All he did was transfer her to another floor, to work in the secretarial pool.

That bothered me. The bitch still worked in his firm, in the same building. It was like Leo was hedging his bets. If it didn't work out between us, he had 18-year-old Lilly right there to replace me.

Leo did pay more attention to me, but it seemed forced at times, and sometimes I still caught him glancing at other girls. It didn't help when I found out his new secretary was another young leggy blonde. I felt at a crossroads, needing to decide if there was a future for us.

A few weeks after the blow-up over Lilly, Danny called and asked me out. I had landed a small part in a new off-Broadway production of *Chicago*, and rehearsal had just ended.

"You know I'm still with Leo," I said.

"You shouldn't be," Danny said. "I told you, you're too good for that loser."

I knew Leo and Danny were rivals in their law firm. My weakness the first time could be excused, because I was so distressed after learning about Leo's affair with Lilly. If I saw Danny again though, I'd really be betraying Leo.

"I don't have anything to change into," I told Danny, looking into the dressing room mirror and seeing my tight Danskin glued to my sweaty body. Then I thought about how Leo had parked Lilly onto a different floor of his law firm, in reserve in case he wanted to replace me. Upgrade to a younger version of me.

I said, "If you don't mind seeing me in sweaty tights and leggings …."

"I'd love to see you in tights and leggings," Danny said with an enthusiastic grin in his voice. I laughed inside. All boys were the same.

Hours later, I opened the door into Leo's study. As always nowadays, he was behind his computer. I knew he read a lot of porn (a lot of hot wife stories), and he barely acknowledged my presence. I dropped my coat and workout bag on the floor and leaned against the door so he could see my profile.

"I saw Danny tonight," I said casually, extending my right leg and nonchalantly tapping the toe of my black ankle strap dance shoe on the floor.

Leo looked up from his screen. "What?"

"Danny. I saw him tonight. After rehearsal." I kept idly tapping my toe, a little to the left, a little to the right. I felt Leo's eyes on my toned legs, I felt his eyes traveling up my body. I knew what he'd see.

He'd see I wasn't wearing the bra top I normally wore – I hadn't put it back on—so he'd also see the outline of my breasts and hard nipples clearly outlined in my tight Danskin. He'd see my hair loose and tousled, not in the neat ponytail I always wore to rehearsal. He'd see my face flushed.

Leo got up from his desk and walked over to me. Standing just inches from me, he cupped my breast, rolling his thumb over my nipple. "What did you do with him?" he asked.

"You know, what friends do," I said.

"You're Danny's friend now?" he asked.

"I am," I said. "We're good friends."

Leo frowned at that, clearly not happy. "I've told you Danny competes with me for clients. He'll do anything to stab me in the back."

I shrugged like that was Leo's problem, not mine.

"You go to a bar with him?" Leo asked.

I shook my head. "His apartment." I moved my foot up his pants leg, pressing the hard toe of my shoe against his ankle.

"His apartment," Leo repeated, as if contemplating the implications. "You're *my* girlfriend. You go to my rival's apartment?"

I shrugged again. "I've been there before," I said, pressing harder into his ankle.

"I thought that was a one-time thing," Leo said.

"Don't worry Leo," I said. "We watched a movie."

It was true. We watched a porno flick as Danny fucked my brains out.

Leo's eyes traveled down my body. I knew what he'd see. A camel toe formed in the crotch of my leotard; the material moist. I felt his finger run between my swollen pussy lips, exploring the wetness in the material.

"Did you cheat on me with Danny?" Leo asked, his voice quivering with excitement.

"I'm your girlfriend," I answered, looking into his eyes. "Why would I cheat on you?"

He caressed my neck, his fingers lightly drawing circles over the hickey Danny had marked me with. Then he pressed his lips against mine, pushing his tongue into my mouth, his hands urgently exploring my body. He threw me onto the sofa and ripped off my clothes.

Just as he was about to plunge into my well used pussy, he looked into my eyes and said, "I love you, Janie!"

I didn't say "I love you" back. I *did* love Leo. He was my life. But I was beginning to realize I had to make him compete for me. I couldn't make it easy for him, or let him get comfortable. I had to keep him on edge. At least until I had a ring on my finger.

———⬤———

MY AFFAIR WITH DANNY went on for 3 months. I never admitted it to Leo – that was the game we were playing. Danny didn't know that Leo knew. And Leo didn't know for sure.

We hooked up 2 or 3 times a week. Danny thought I was pretty, sexy ... he loved fucking me.

Danny could have any girl though. He was handsome and successful. What he really loved about fucking me, was I was Leo's girlfriend. Every time he fucked me, he was fucking over Leo too. Every time he fucked me, he was winning against Leo.

Danny said he loved me. He said I should break up with Leo and move in with him.

I didn't believe him. He wanted me to break up with Leo to get the ultimate victory against his rival. It didn't matter anyways. I didn't love Danny.

I loved Leo, despite all his kinky desires. Outside our sex life, he remained the kind gentle man I'd fallen in love with. And now, once again, he was lavishing me with his attention and warmth. He stopped looking at other girls. I was the center of his world. He adored me again.

Then everything changed. Again.

I found out I was pregnant. I was on the pill. But I got pregnant anyways.

I never made Leo wear a condom. Or Danny. I was having regular sex with both of them. I didn't know who the father was.

I didn't know what to do. I should have just gotten an abortion and never let Leo know. But I found it impossible to do that. I had become too dependent on him. I was frozen, unable to act. I couldn't make the decision to end the pregnancy without telling him. It was like South Beach all over again. I needed Leo to save me.

I guess it didn't surprise me when lust filled Leo's eyes as I told him I was pregnant. He knew the baby might be Danny's. We never mentioned him—we were still playing the game where Leo didn't know about my affair with his work rival.

Leo even jokingly said, "Well, I guess what they say is right, condoms aren't foolproof."

Leo's joke made me cry. How could he joke about this? This wasn't a game anymore. I was pregnant. This was a baby we were talking about.

Leo immediately pulled me into his arms and comforted me. For a moment he stepped out of the game and said, "I'll love this baby, as much as I love you. You're my life. I'll always take care of you and the baby."

Leo's promise made me cry even harder, but in a good way. It reminded me why I loved him despite all the craziness. It reminded me why he was my Prince Charming.

We made love three times that night. Leo couldn't get enough of me. I knew why. I was cheating on him. His rival with the handsome face, gorgeous body, and beautiful cock was fucking me right under his nose. And he may have gotten me pregnant. I wondered if Leo *hoped* the baby was Danny's. Was that his ultimate fantasy, for another man – his rival – to impregnate the girl he loved?

The next day, Leo asked me to marry him. Despite everything, I couldn't help being overjoyed. I bawled as he put his engagement ring on my finger, and the people around us at *Per Se* applauded and cheered. We told our parents, and they couldn't have been more happy for us. We also told them I was pregnant, and they didn't seem to mind (of course, we gave no clue the father might not be Leo). We wanted the wedding to happen before I started showing, so it was planned for two months from now.

For the next 3 weeks I avoided Danny. I didn't want to see him. I'm sure he knew about my engagement to Leo, and I didn't want to have to go through the charade of breaking up with him. I was hoping he'd get the message and go away, but to my dismay he texted me and left voice mails constantly. He said he loved me; he wanted me to dump Leo and marry him.

Was that possible? Had Danny really fallen in love with me? Our affair wasn't just a way for him to fuck over Leo, his rival in the law firm?

One evening at dinner, Leo said, "You know, I ran into Danny today. He's in a bad way. Do you know what could be bothering him?"

"Um—no, I have no idea," I sputtered, not sure where Leo was going with this.

Leo looked into my eyes. "Well, I know the two of you are friends. I thought you might want to have lunch with him. Maybe you can help him with his problem."

I looked incredulously at Leo. His message was clear. He wanted me to continue my *secret* affair with Danny. I guess it didn't really surprise me.

A part of me thought it was wrong. We were engaged, and I was pregnant. But I hadn't really believed Leo would change. And what about me? To be honest, I missed the sex with Danny. I wasn't lying to Leo when I said Danny was better than him in bed.

I felt moisture between my legs. "Well, okay," I finally said in a resigned, but excited voice. "I'll call him tomorrow."

My affair with Danny continued until right before the wedding. He fucked me all the time, sometimes every day. Once he fucked me in his office, as I could hear Leo speaking just outside the locked door. Another time he fucked me against the wall in an alley outside a restaurant, while Leo sat inside at our table, waiting for me to return from the ladies room.

I never told Danny I was pregnant. I didn't want to deal with that.

A few days before the wedding, Leo casually mentioned that Danny had been transferred to their Minnesota office. That surprised me, because Minnesota was the office they sent lawyers who had no future with the law firm.

Later, I quietly checked around and discovered Leo had arranged for Danny's transfer. I couldn't help admiring Leo. In the end, he had proven who was the true Alpha Male. That night, I fucked Leo's brains out, and came twice on his cock.

I felt a little sorry for Danny, but not too much. I knew he'd be able to easily get another job making kazillions a year. I missed him as a lover though. He had a gorgeous face and hot body, and he could take me places sexually that Leo never approached.

We honeymooned in the Bahamas. I wasn't showing yet, so my tummy was still flat and the rest of my body tight and toned from dancing. I tan easily, so it took just a day to make my body a golden brown. The ocean saltwater and sun made my natural blonde hair even blonder.

I paraded around the pool and resort in skimpy bikinis and flirty sundresses like I owned the place. Now married with a wedding ring around my finger, my ego and self-esteem were at an all time high.

I couldn't stop looking at my wedding ring and my engagement ring with its huge diamond, and I loved all the attention my new husband lavished upon me. I was in nirvana, and so was Leo. He loved the lustful stares I got from other men, and whenever I wanted to drive him even more out of his mind with desire, I only had to bring his hand to my tummy.

We were lounging by the pool when a bunch of hunky guys jumped in and played a rowdy game of water basketball. I wore a skimpy white bikini that showed off my tan, and that was just sheer enough to hint at my dark nipples and areolas when wet. My tits were still tiny of course, but in the string bikinis Leo picked out for me, men seemed unable to take their eyes off them.

The guys kept glancing my way as they played. I pretended not to notice, but Leo was paying close attention. After a few minutes he looked at me. "I think I'll head up to the room for a while and check my email." Then he looked back at the guys in the pool, inviting me to look back with him.

I recognized the expression on his face, and the tone of his voice. He wanted to play the game. I tilted my head in surprise. "Really? Are you sure?"

"Yes, I'm positive." His voice burned with excitement, and lust filled his eyes.

I watched him walk away, and then thought for a moment. The thought of playing the game on our honeymoon, just days after saying our wedding vows, sent a wicked shiver down my spine. And I hadn't gotten fucked really good since Danny moved to Minnesota.

After a few minutes, I got up and stepped into the far side of the pool, well away from the basketball game. The guys threw the ball back and forth, moving in my direction, and soon they surrounded me.

The basketball game continued, but now I was in the middle of it.

"Hey!" I laughed as someone splashed me with water. Up to that point I was wet only up to my tummy. Now I was soaked everywhere.

"Sorry," the guilty guy said, his eyes on my wet bikini top and what it might be revealing. Then another guy splashed more water on me.

"If you don't like the water, get out of the pool!" he said laughing. I laughed and splashed back, and soon we were in a full-fledged water battle. They invited me to play in their basketball game, which turned into a "let's grope the pretty blonde girl as much as possible" game. We were all laughing and having a good time.

One of the guys, Anton, was particular hunky—out of this world gorgeous, really—so I invited him to sit next to me. "Just toss that on the ground," I said pointing to the magazine Leo had been reading.

"Where's your husband?" Anton asked as he carelessly threw the magazine onto the wet pool deck, soaking and ruining it.

"I don't know," I said in an uncaring voice. "Email I think."

"I heard you got married just last week? Man, if I had a hot wife like you, I wouldn't let her out of my sight."

"Are you flirting with me?" I said laughing, and he laughed too. "Honestly, though, I don't mind when he's away."

"What do you mean by that?" he asked looking intrigued.

I shrugged, then picked up the Coppertone and rubbed lotion over my long legs. As I bent at the waist to lather my calves, my wet bikini top fell away slightly, giving him a clear view of my A-cup breasts. Sitting back up, I looked at him and smiled. Then I stretched out onto my belly, glancing fleeting at his crotch. He had an erection (and a nice big one too). I rested my head on my crossed arms and closed my eyes. "Can you put lotion on my back?"

He bolted out of his chair and sat next to me on mine. Then I felt his hands on my back, rubbing lotion across my soft tanned skin. It felt good. His hands were large and strong and calloused, so different from Leo's. "What do you mean, you don't mind when your husband's away?" Anton asked again.

I noticed the people around us eavesdropping on our conversation. "Shhhh," I whispered. I reached behind me and pulled the bottom string of my top. "Can you rub here? Last year I got burnt."

"Listen," he said in a low voice as he enthusiastically rubbed lotion on my back. "My friends are going clubbing tonight. If you're looking for some fun—"

God his hands felt good. I could tell this wasn't the first time he'd given a girl a massage. Feeling naughtier by the second, I reached back and pulled the top string of my bikini, the one around my neck. "Here too, okay?" I said, his hands on my neck as soon as the words left my lips. "Wait," I said, pulling my blonde hair to the side. He started again on my neck. Then his fingers went up and down my bare back, from my neck to just above my butt crack, his movement more sensual than massaging.

Without my asking or permission, he started on my legs, moving from the edge of my bikini bottoms to the soles of my feet. I didn't stop him. The way he slowly and carefully worked my thighs and calves, I knew he was a leg man.

"Man, your legs are toned!" he gushed, confirming my suspicion.

"I'm a dancer," I murmured, opening my legs slightly. He noticed, and his hands moved up my inner thighs. I'm sure he noticed the moisture in the crotch of my bikini bottoms.

"You dance in a strip club?" he teased. I could hear the smile on his face.

"Broadway, you jerk," I replied pretending to be angry. "I'm in *Chicago*."

"*Chicago*, huh? Are you one of those dancers who wears a garter belt and stockings?"

Suddenly my cell rang. Holding my top across my breasts with one hand, I reached for the phone with my other. "It's my husband," I said looking at the caller-id. I listened to Leo for a minute, then re-tied my top. "I've got to go," I said to Anton.

Anton grabbed my hand as I got up. "Tonight?" he asked.

I'm sure he saw the indecision on my face. "How can I contact you?" I finally said, whispering.

Smiling, he grabbed the cell from my hand and dialed a number. I heard a ringing from his cell. "I just called myself," he said. "Now you've got my number on your phone."

I nodded.

"So, you'll come?" he asked.

"Yes."

"Yes, you'll come?" he said excitedly.

I smiled teasingly. "Yes, I'm one of those girls in *Chicago* who wears stockings."

I rushed off, a big smile on my face. Entering the hotel lobby, I went into the gift shop and bought a red baseball cap and a pair of sunglasses. Then I went to our room.

I found Leo in the room working on his computer. I came up behind him and put my arms around his neck, affectionately kissing the top of his head. "Hi honey, what're you doing?" I asked.

"Work, what else? Another client emergency."

"Oh," I said. Contrary to what he said, I saw he was surfing the *Loving Wives* section of *Literotica*.

Walking to the sofa, I casually took off my bikini and tossed it onto the cushion, as if getting ready to take a shower. I pretended to be thinking about something, avoiding his eyes, but I made sure I was in his field of vision, making it easy for him to see my erect nipples, my flushed cheeks, my swelling pussy lips, all signs he knew marked my sexual arousal. I stepped into my black high heels, walking here and there, as if trying them on for the first time.

"What are you doing?" he asked looking amused and intrigued.

I giggled. "I don't know, just daydreaming I guess, thinking about what to wear for dinner."

He got up and put his arms around me. "I'm sorry, honey, but I think I'll need to work tonight. There's a big deadline tomorrow. Why don't you go without me?"

I feigned disappointment. "Well ... I think I heard the guys at the pool say they were going to a club tonight."

Leo shrugged, pretending to look back at his computer screen. "That sounds like fun," he said trying to sound uninterested, but I heard excitement in his voice.

"Um, could you do something for me first?" I asked grabbing his hand. I led him to the bed. Still wearing the black heels, I got on top of him, moving up his body until I straddled his face.

"Do you mind?" I asked, lowering my pussy onto his face.

Leo eagerly lapped at my damp pussy, his hands moving up my toned thighs and down my tight ass. Putting my hands on his head to steady myself, I closed my eyes and remembered the pool, how I practically undressed for Anton, how he rubbed and caressed my body and then asked me out, how I so scandalously did this in front of so many people, people who likely knew I was a newly married bride on my honeymoon, and how I had retreated from Anton with my nipples erect and my bikini bottoms damp, their disapproving eyes on me, whispering to each other how I was such a dirty cheating wife.

I pushed and gyrated against Leo mouth, silently urging him to lick hard against my clit and to stick his tongue into my pussy. After the pool I desperately needed some release before seeing Anton and his friends again.

Sensing I was close to the edge, Leo rapidly flicked the tip of his tongue over my clit, just the way he knew drives me wild. My body tensed and then shuddered, and I mercilessly pushed and rubbed my pussy against Leo's face, wanting to lengthen and intensify my orgasm. Even after my orgasm subsided, I remained planted on my new husband's face, catching my breath. Finally, I got off him, letting my heels drop off my feet and hit the floor.

His face was wet from my moisture. His pants sported a huge tent. Normally I'd reciprocate now and give him pleasure, but tonight was different. He started this after all. I turned and started for the shower.

"Ah, honey, my turn?" he said, pointing to his pants.

I gave him a mischievous look and laughed playfully. "You don't want me to be late, do you?"

I leaned in to kiss him, but at the last moment teasingly pulled away. I gripped his balls just hard enough to make him wince. "Don't you dare play with yourself," I warned. "I have plans for you tonight."

I stepped away and eyed my new husband. "If I think you jerked off while I'm away, I might have to put your little cock in a cage."

Leo moaned at my words. I couldn't help laughing.

I showered and came back into the room wearing my robe. Leo pretended to work at his computer, but in reality watched my every move. I felt like an actress playing a role. Paying no attention to him, I fixed my hair and put on more make up than usual (he loves it when I wear heavy makeup). With that done, I dropped my robe and rubbed moisturizer all over my body, spending extra time on my long legs and pretty feet. Then I put on my pink Jimmy Choo strappy high heels. It had 4-inch pencil thin heels and two leather straps, one over my toes (freshly painted pink), and the other around my ankles.

I sauntered around the room pretending to think about what to wear, but in reality I had already decided. I knew Leo loved to see me nude in stiletto heels.

Finally, I put on my chosen dress. Leo bought it for me before the wedding. It was light pink and tied in a bow in the back. It was snug from my shoulders to waist, but at my waist the skirt flared out and ended around mid-thigh. If I danced at all the skirt could easily fly above the parts of me that only my husband should see, but that wasn't what made the dress outrageous. What made the dress obscene was its material, which was fine in normal light, but in strobe lights the dress became practically transparent.

I kissed Leo and opened the door. "I bought you a little present" I said pointing to the bag on the bed as I disappeared out the door.

At the club Anton's hands were all over me, but I managed to keep it decent. He repeatedly tried to drag me to the dance floor, but I hesitated, trying to buy time.

Finally, I saw a man among the crowd, wearing a red hat and sunglasses. With a slight smile, I took Anton's hand and let him lead me to the dance floor. I gently nudged him to the side of the club where Red Hat was standing. We started dancing facing each other, with Anton trying to put his arms around me. I kept him at a distance, enjoying the music and twirling back and forth. With each twirl my skirt ballooned, revealing more of my legs and sometimes the curve of my behind, making the people watching wonder if I had gone commando (in fact, I had worn a lacy pink g-string).

Strobe lights pulsed through the high energy dance floor, each intense flash rendering my dress practically transparent and momentarily revealing my body to the hungry male eyes around us. Anton's eyes were lust filled, as were those of the men watching us.

Red Hat wore sunglasses so I couldn't see his reaction, but I knew what he wanted. I turned and then leaned into Anton, pressing my back against his front, feeling his hard cock between my butt cheeks. Anton's hands were on my hips, and as we swayed to the music, I raised my arms behind me and around Anton's neck.

I closed my eyes as the strobe lights revealed my body to Red Hat and the other men watching. I felt Anton's lips on my cheek, and I turned my head and parted my lips, inviting his tongue into my mouth. Then I felt Anton's hands move up my body and cup my breasts, denying the sight of my nipples and areolas from Red Hat, but treating him to a more erotic show as my new lover cupped and fondled me.

A couple hours later I returned to our suite at the resort. Leo sat in the bed. I probably looked freshly fucked to him. He eagerly beckoned me to join him, and as soon as I sat down, he kissed me and smelled my hair. He must have liked what he found because his cock grew harder against my side.

"I finished work early, so I went looking for you," he said.

"Really? Too bad you couldn't find us."

"Yeah, too bad. But I had an interesting time." Leo laid me down and got on top of me. "There was a girl there, a good looking blonde. You should have seen her; you could see right through her dress. She practically fucked the guy she was with on the dance floor in front of everyone."

Leo pushed my dress up around my waist. He stopped talking to look at me. My panties were gone, and a thick milky fluid oozed between my swollen pussy lips.

"What happen then?" I asked as I unzipped his fly and pulled out his hard penis. I grabbed his shaft and guided him towards me.

"She went with him into the alley behind the club," Leo said entering me. "I followed with a bunch of other guys. We watched as he fucked her up against the wall."

"Oh god," I moaned as Leo fucked me. "His dick must've been really long if he could fuck her standing up."

Leo paused, looking at me inquiringly. "Really?" he asked.

"Yeah," I breathed. "Otherwise, he'd fall out of her."

Leo considered my words. "I guess it might be hard for me to do you that way."

"Why do you think we always do missionary, or me on top?" I asked.

Leo stared at me. His face was covered in lust, and he looked like he was going to have a heart attack.

"Tell me what happened next," I said.

"He fucked her so hard he practically lifted her out of her heels. He probably would have, if she hadn't been wearing ankle strap heels." I pressed the stilettos of my ankle strap heels into my husband's calves.

"She had fantastic legs!" Leo gushed. "She wrapped one leg around his thigh, like she was begging him to go deeper inside her. Did I tell you she didn't make him wear a condom?"

"Maybe it didn't matter if he came inside her. Maybe she was already pregnant," I said, bringing Leo's hands to my tummy.

"Oh god!" he gasped as he came. I wasn't going to cum again, not after the orgasms Anton gave me earlier.

Leo spooned me and whispered sweet nothings to me. I felt happy and secure. I was married. My husband adored me, and he was successful. Men desired me; they thought I was pretty and sexy. And Leo couldn't get enough of me.

I had never been so happy in my life.

PREGNANCY WAS HARD. Morning sickness hit me soon after our honeymoon. I couldn't dance and had to leave the cast of Chicago, which broke my heart. But after 9 months I gave birth to a wonderful baby boy, who I instantly adored. True to his word, Leo was a wonderful father. We named the baby Leonard Jr.

About three months after giving birth, Leo called and said he was bringing an important new client home for dinner. His name was Edward. I hurriedly got ready. I'd gone from size 2 to 4 during the pregnancy and hadn't yet lost the extra weight. I couldn't wear my slinkiest dresses, but there were a few outfits that fit.

We hadn't played the game at all since the honeymoon, and our sex life was almost non-existent. I suspected Leo wanted me to play the game with Edward, so I dressed to impress. I knew what turned Leo on, and I didn't want his wandering eye to re-emerge. Also, despite my new role as the mother of a newborn, which I cherished, I missed the wild kinky sex from before.

Edward was older, probably early 50s, but he was handsome and distinguished, and looked fit under his expensive Italian suit. And he was black!

Leo didn't waste any time. As we sat on the sofa sipping wine, with Edward sitting on a chair across from us, Leo began caressing my neck and shoulder, and then started kissing me. I felt movement next to me and realized Edward had joined us on the sofa. It became clear to me that Leo and Edward talked about this already, and Edward knew he had Leo's permission.

Soon Edward's hands were on me, and Leo moved to the chair to watch as Edward fondled and kissed me. Edward took off my dress, leaving me in just my lingerie and heels. I wanted to turn off the light, embarrassed by the bulges in my stomach and hips, but Leo wouldn't allow it as he wanted to watch.

Edward took off his clothes. For an older man he kept in shape. His body was lean and well-defined and very black. Jet black.

Edward's penis was an impressive size, one of the longest I'd ever seen. And thick. It was the first black cock I'd ever seen (other than in adult movies). I'd say his was a stereotypical big black cock.

I grimaced when Edward penetrated me. I wasn't used to his size. But he was patient and took his time with me. Eventually he was all the way inside me, and the stretching sensations I felt turned from pain to pleasure.

It felt good as Edward moved inside me. While not as energetic as a younger man, he was an experienced, considerate lover. I didn't make him wear a condom because I was back on the pill. As Edward fucked me, I looked over at Leo, who was excitedly beating off.

I came really hard on Edward's BBC. He came hard too and flooded my pussy with his sperm. With my legs still over Edward's shoulders, I looked over at my husband. Leo was panting hard. His hand was covered with the spunk of his orgasm. And yes, I did notice the small size of Leo's softening manhood compared to Edward's which was still inside me (and still big even though his was softening too).

Leo encouraged me to have a relationship with Edward. Edward's wife had died the year before and he had been looking for a younger girl to spend time with. He wanted great sex and a little romance, but not anything serious like marriage (he wasn't ready for that).

This seemed to be a new wrinkle on Leo's fantasy. With Danny and Anton, I'd been the cheating girlfriend/fiancée/wife, having secret affairs behind Leo's back. Now with Edward, Leo wanted me to have not just a physical but also an emotional relationship with another man. I'd read enough stories on *Literotica* and other sites like *ourhotwives* to know this was a variation on the hot wife/cuckold fantasy. I didn't see any harm in it. I'd get great sex with Edward and satisfy Leo's fantasies at the same time.

And while I liked Edward, there wasn't any chance I'd fall in love with him, which was exactly the relationship Edward wanted. So, when Edward called a few days later and asked me out, I accepted.

"I loved watching you dance in *Chicago*," Edward said as we sipped a cocktail before dinner.

"You saw me?" I asked surprised.

"Didn't Leo tell you? He showed me a video of the production, from about a year ago. I know this is a terrible thing to say, but that's when I decided to hire Leo as my attorney. After he told me about this game you play, and how he'd be willing to share you with me, well ... honestly I couldn't resist, you're extraordinarily beautiful."

My cheeks reddened with embarrassment. "You must think we're so demented."

"It's unconventional, that's for sure," he said laughing, but not in an unkind way. Then he looked admiringly at me. "My god you're absolutely gorgeous."

Edward's unabashed praise made me blush. I thought about how much my life had changed. Back in high school, boys wouldn't give me the time of day unless I opened my legs for them. Now, men found me beautiful and desirable. Why? Was it because I was older and more sure of myself? Was that the key to beauty? Good self-esteem?

Then I thought of the baby weight I hadn't yet lost. "I'm not as pretty as when you saw me in Chicago."

He smiled lecherously at me, the lust so apparent in his eyes it sent a shiver down my spine. "Come home with me, and I'll show you how beautiful and sexy I think you are."

I went home with him. That's when I realized how rich he was, as his home was a huge condo in an ultra-exclusive building bordering Central Park. He fucked me twice, and Leo fucked me again when I got home.

I went out with Edward 2 or 3 times a week. Sometimes I spent the night with him, or even the weekend. He liked taking me to society parties. Leo loved that I was spending so much time with Edward. Sometimes we'd go out as a threesome. If you saw us, you'd have thought I was married to Edward, not Leo. It was a naughty thrill to hold Edward's hand and whisper sweet nothings into his ear as Leo sat across from us, looking both hurt and excited at the same time.

I found it amazing how perverted high society gentlemen could be. Leo was certainly that way, with his hot wife/cuckold fantasies. But Edward and his friends were just as bad.

Things were proper when their wives were around of course. At those times, I didn't wear my wedding ring since it would have been scandalous if his high society friends knew he was dating a married woman (miraculously I never ran into anyone I knew when I was with Edward, but then, we ran in different circles).

Sometimes, though, Edward took me to his private club, where things often got wild.

Edward's club catered to rich, powerful black men. Almost all of them had young pretty white girls on their arms. Edward insisted I wear my wedding ring at his club, because he wanted all his black friends to know he was fucking a young *married* white woman.

He liked me to wear my most revealing dresses around his friends. But unlike Leo, he had no interest in sharing me. I guess it was a *"my girl is sexier than yours"* kind of thing. He loved telling his friends I was a dancer on Broadway and most recently performed in *Chicago*.

Edward openly fondled me in front of his friends. He'd inch my dress up as we danced, grinning over my shoulder to his friends as he revealed the lacy tops of my stockings. One time he even made me go down on him under the table, as he smoked a Cuban cigar and drank expensive single malt scotch with his friends.

I went along with it. I still hadn't lost the extra weight from my pregnancy, and I'd had no luck getting a part in another show.

I loved Leonard and being a mom, but as I've described, my self-esteem has always been an issue for me. Leo helped, but the fact he'd always been crazy about me didn't help. It was kind of like *"well, I'm with you, of course you have to say that."*

Edward was different. He was someone new. His adoration of my body and looks, as well as being hit on constantly by his friends (all of whom were handsome and successful – and black), satisfied some primal need inside me. Also, the taboo of Edward – a black man – added an edgy wickedness to our relationship.

Me with Edward also kept Leo focused on me, although I still worried about his wandering eye for young pretty girls, especially with all the time we spent apart. Was he using my evenings and weekends with Edward as opportunities to be with younger, firmer girls (whose bodies had not gone through the rigors of childbirth)? It didn't seem that way, as he was always there when I got home, practically panting with excitement and begging me to tell him about my latest adventures with Edward. The idea of my dating another man, having a boyfriend, turned Leo on. It made him jealous too, but the jealousy fueled his excitement.

Edward was handsome, distinguished, charming and charismatic in a way that could only be gained after years as a successful businessman. I looked forward to our dates and found myself daydreaming about him when we weren't together.

This alarmed me. I didn't want to fall in love with him. Loving two men would be too complicated.

Predictably, Leo was thrilled as he saw my relationship with Edward blossom. To him it would be the ultimate cuckold fantasy if I fell in love with Edward.

Still, the hurt I saw in my Leo's face as I got ready for another date with Edward bothered me, even though I knew it was part of his fantasy. So, despite all the wonderful things about Edward, I started thinking about breaking it off with him.

Then my life turned upside down again. I missed my next period, and the doctor confirmed I was pregnant.

How was this possible? I was on the pill. How could this happen again?

We told Edward. We had no choice. This wasn't like Danny. I was in a relationship with Edward.

There was another reason this wasn't Danny. A big reason. With Danny, I wasn't sure if the baby was his or Leo's. I still didn't know who Leonard's biological father was. We'd never done a paternity test.

But now, I was certain the father was Edward. I was with Edward two or three (or 4) nights a week, and he never used a condom or pulled out, and he always came a lot.

I was having a lot of sex with Leo too. But lately, it was more pillow talk (about my latest adventures with Edward) while Leo slowly masturbated. It was kind of a way of denying Leo. He was into that. I never put his cock in a cage. But my mouth and pussy were off-limits, reserved only for Edward.

The knowledge that Edward was probably the father of the baby in my tummy sent me reeling. How were we going to deal with this? A half-black baby. What would we say to our parents? Our friends?

Then all of a sudden, Edward got possessive. He didn't have any children. He wasn't like Danny, who didn't care. Danny sort of knew he might be the father of Leonard, but he never said anything – he didn't want the responsibility.

Edward was different. He wanted to be the father. And he wanted the mother of his baby – me! – to be his wife. He started putting pressure on me to divorce Leo and marry him.

I wasn't going to do that. I didn't love Edward. I loved Leo. It didn't help, though, that Leo got off on the idea of losing me to Edward. It was another one of his cuckold fantasies.

And then things really got crazy. Edward hired a private investigator to look into things. The fact I'd gotten pregnant twice while on the pill was suspicious.

The private investigator uncovered a terrible truth. Leo substituted my birth control bills for placebos! *He wanted me to get bred by other men!*

I was devastated. At that point, I had no choice. I left Leo and moved in with Edward. Edward's attorney started divorce proceedings. I agreed to marry Edward. We decided to have the wedding after I gave birth to the baby. Tests showed the baby in my stomach *was* Edward's. 9 months later I gave birth to a half-black baby – Edward Jr.

EPILOGUE – 1 YEAR LATER

"So, how are you Leo?" I asked my ex-husband as we exchanged Leonard. Leo got our child every other weekend.

Leo shrugged. He looked sad and resigned. He said, "Good, I guess."

"Seeing anyone?" I asked.

"You know," Leo said with another shrug. He joked, "A couple barely legal girls." We both laughed.

"Are you happy with Edward?" Leo asked.

"I am," I said. It was true. Life with Edward was good. He was a great husband, and an amazing father. "I got a part in *Hamilton*."

"Wow. That's amazing, Janie. Congrats," Leo said.

I smiled and said, "It's just a little part, I don't have any lines, but thanks."

We were silent for long moments. It was a sad, melancholy moment.

Finally, I said, "Leo, I don't know if I've ever told you. Or told you enough. But you save me. You really did. You were my Prince Charming."

Leo smiled sheepishly, looking humble. Looking at his feet, he joked, "I guess I turned out to be just a frog."

We both laughed.

Getting serious again, I said, "I'll always love you, Leo. I'll always be there for you."

Leo looked hopeful. "Really?" he said.

"Yeah, I mean ... yeah," I said. It was true. Since married to Edward, I'd had a lot of time to think. I owed Leo a lot. I owed him my life. My happiness. He'd gone too far, way too far. But still. Time heals wounds. I owed him. And at some level, I did still love him.

"I miss you," Leo said. In a pleading voice, he said, "Maybe we can be friends."

"I'd like that," I said back.

Then we smiled at each other for long moments. After a while, we squeezed hands, and then we parted, going our separate ways.

I sensed, though, my life with Leo was not over. And it wasn't just because we shared a child, Leonard. I didn't know what the future would bring. But I was certain it would include Leo.

Because he was, in some ways, still my Prince Charming.

Don't miss out!

Visit the website below and you can sign up to receive emails whenever Pete Andrews publishes a new book. There's no charge and no obligation.

https://books2read.com/r/B-A-KWSAB-AIZWC

BOOKS 2 READ

Connecting independent readers to independent writers.

Also by Pete Andrews

Be Careful What You Wish For
Be Careful What You Wish For Book 1
A Cuckold Fiancée and a Cuckquean Wife - Be Careful What You Wish For Book 2
My Girl Is Another Man's Date - Be Careful What You Wish For Book 3
My Fiancee Skin-To-Skin With Another Man - Be Careful What You Wish For Book 4
Groom Watches New Bride With Another Man - Be Careful What You Wish For Book 5
Bride With Rival On Honeymoon - Be Careful What You Wish For Book 6

Faithful Wife's Fall From Grace
Faithful Wife's Fall From Grace Book 1
Faithful Wife's Fall From Grace Book 2
Faithful Wife's Fall From Grace Book 3
Faithful Wife's Fall From Grace Book 4
Faithful Wife's Fall From Grace Book 5
Faithful Wife's Fall From Grace Book 6
Faithful Wife's Fall From Grace Book 7
Faithful Wife's Fall From Grace Book 8

Flash Of Stocking Collection
Wife Watching Game And Other Stories: Flash of Stocking
Collection 1
Wife Dates Another Man and Other Stories: Flash of Stocking
Collection 2
Losing My Wife To Another Man - Three Interracial Cuckold
Novellas: Flash of Stocking Collection 3

Girls Who Belong To Other Men
Girls Who Belong To Other Men Book 1
Girls Who Belong To Other Men Book 2

Opening Pandora's Box
Opening Pandora's Box 1 - Jessie Plays For Her Husband
Opening Pandora's Box 2 - Ollie Watches His Wife With Another
Man
Opening Pandora's Box 3 - Jessie Grows Closer To Roman
Opening Pandora's Box 4 - Jessie Loses Herself In Roman
Opening Pandora's Box 5 - How Can You Do This To Me?

Tiny Dancer: A Modern Romance
Tiny Dancer: A Young Cuckold Romance Book 1
Tiny Dancer: A Modern Romance Book 2
Tiny Dancer: A Young Cuckold Romance Book 3

Standalone

Playing At Work Is Dangerous: A Reluctant Wife Story